His One and Only

Steel Security #2

Charity Parkerson

Punk & Sissy Publications

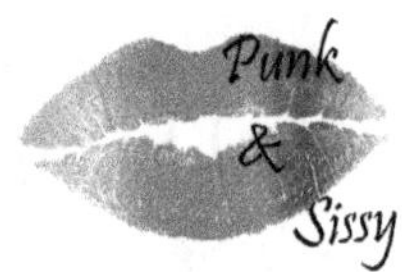

—Warning: This book is intended for readers over the age of 18. Some of my books contain allusions to past abuse and trauma.

Editor: BZ Hercules & Consultants

Cover art: Temptations Creations

RIGHT

DING, AND distribut-
the internet or via
ıout the permission
r is illegal and pun-
uthor and/or pub-
permission to use
. This includes the
g into AI systems.
ingement, includ-
ut monetary gain,
BI and is punish-

Contents

Introduction

Two men with equally big secrets. Both desperate to hide the truth. This rockstar and bodyguard are about to explode—one way or another.

When Valon made it big in the music industry, it wasn't a dream come true for him. His fame is for the people who pushed him to the top. All Valon saw was his escape. Now Valon is trapped in another life that's slowly killing him. All the ways he's found to cope will definitely see him dead in a back alley someday. The entire situation has him drowning with no hope of survival... until Marc.

As much as Marc would like to claim he wasn't one of Valon's biggest fans, he was. His celebrity crush has only gotten worse since becoming the star's bodyguard. He knows exactly how amazing Valon is now, and the obsession is twice as deep. But Valon is hiding something. Something big. Marc won't stop until he uncovers the truth behind Valon's downward spiral. No matter what it is, Marc has just what he needs to find happiness.

His One and Only is the second book in Charity Parkerson's Steel Security series. These showcase some of the toughest bodyguards in the country as they fall hard for men they never see coming.

Author Note

This one includes past abuse and current trauma.

Chapter One

Sweat rolled down Marc's body. He gasped for air. He honestly had no idea what had convinced him he could simply take up jogging at the grand old age of thirty. That wasn't true. Valon had suggested it. Marc was the muscle. He wasn't built for speed. Marc had played football years ago. He had never been part of the track team. Now he wondered if he might die.

"Fucking Valon." Even as he growled the words, his aggravation transformed. Damn. He was sexy. No doubt Marc had been lost staring into his navy-blue eyes when Valon had told Marc he should take up jogging so he could keep up with Valon. Admittedly, Valon was a pretty active guy. Sometimes he exhausted the hell out of Marc. Marc lived for every second of it. Not only was Valon hot as fuck with his shoulder-length curly silver hair, but he was also the lead singer of Backlash. That was Marc's favorite band. He had already been a little obsessed with Valon before they had met. Now Valon knew Marc. Marc wasn't a lost face in a sea of concertgoers. He had the perfect job at the feet of greatness. Marc had to do whatever it took to keep Valon.

The loud honk of a too-close car came from nowhere. Marc jumped and spun, ready to fight even as his heart tried to burst from his chest.

Valon's bright smile immediately calmed him. He pulled up next to Marc and rolled down the window. "Get in, loser. You'll never make it back home."

Why did it have to be *the* Valon Stark watching him fail? "I'm good." God, everything screamed in agony.

Valon rolled his eyes.

Marc thanked every deity he was too winded to whimper. Those eyes were so sexy, especially lined in dark eyeliner the way they were now.

"Get in. I'm hungry. Let's get you back to the house so you can snag a quick shower. We're going out for the day."

With that amazing excuse saving him, Marc didn't hesitate to climb into the two-hundred-thousand-dollar SUV. Before Marc had agreed to this assignment, Valon had been on thin ice with Steel Security, where Marc worked. Valon had fired or forced almost every guard on the payroll to quit. His entire file was marked in red because he was impossible to work with. He constantly sneaked away. Screamed every time he didn't get his way and was just generally horrible. So far, Marc had been with Valon for three months, and none of that had gone down. Of course, Marc had approached Valon's needs a lot differently than his previous guards had done. Marc loved going along with Valon to every tiny thing he wanted to do—which was a lot. Valon still sneaked away, but he didn't know Marc was completely aware and followed him, staying in the shadows. Because of his stealth and agreeable nature, Valon treated him like the friend Marc had hoped they could be. Marc wanted to stay in Valon's life. Valon needed way more protection than anyone understood. Marc knew him and never wanted to be anywhere else again.

"Where are we headed for lunch today?" Marc threw some excitement into his tone, wanting Valon to know he was happy to do whatever.

Valon chuckled. "I'm sure you've worked up an appetite."

Even though Valon watched the road, Marc shrugged. "It's not that. I mean, yeah, I'm starved. But I grew up lower-middle class, and it shows now. Like, we never went without or anything, but we always had food at home if I asked to go anywhere. Forget ever going on any big shopping trips. My best friend had a mom who did everything with him. Sometimes, she'd pick us up from school, buy us iced coffee and we'd hit all the popular discount stores. She always tried to buy things for me, but I knew my mom would be pissed if I let anyone spend their hard-earned money on me." Marc had no idea why he always said so much to Valon. Once he started, he couldn't stop. Today was no different. "Being with you makes me feel like I have those days back, but I can buy things for myself without fear."

Valon flashed a bright smile his way. "It makes me happy being with you too. I'm so glad Kash asked you to take me on as a client. We've been great together." He took Marc's hand and squeezed. "I totally get what you're saying about the shopping trips. Dad and I used to do the same things. Of course, those trips were always ruined by Ry. Anytime he found out we had done anything, he would scream at Dad about wasting his money on his worthless son." Valon shrugged, as if those memories didn't hurt.

Marc couldn't look away. He also couldn't imagine having a parent who hated him. While his parents had been strict and thrifty, he had always known he was loved. Truth be told, that kind of fucked with his head, knowing everything he knew about them now. But they were talking about Ry, not his dad.

"That guy's a piece of shit."

A bark of laughter burst from Valon. "Yeah. How did that go for him, though? I hit it big and get to willingly spoil my dad now. He ended up alone and bald. Of course, he tries to pretend he wasn't abusive now, but nope. I'm never letting that shit go. He'll never get anything out of me I give freely out of love. It's in my ironclad will that he never sees a single penny of my money." He chuckled. "In fact, I've ordered my attorney to sue Ry if he ever tries to claim he's any relation to me in public."

Marc snorted so hard, it hurt. A cackle followed. There was no controlling the sound. “Remind me never to get on your bad side. You choose violence.”

Valon never stopped smiling. “Oh, I’m fully self-aware that I’m a petty Betty, but fuck that guy. He’s a monster.”

The laughter died an immediate death inside Marc. He had never heard Valon go quite that far when it came to Ry. It didn’t matter if Valon still smiled. There had been something dark behind that statement.

“Oh.” Valon jumped slightly. “I never answered your question. We’re going to Dad’s to eat. He’s grilling steaks, and we’ll be swimming and all that. So make sure you bring your swim trunks. I fully expect you to be in the pool, keeping me from drowning.” The way Valon laughed made Marc shake his head. Valon knew he had Marc wrapped around his little finger. That was fine. Marc was thrilled to be there.

Going to his dad's house always had Valon fighting mixed feelings. There honestly was no one Valon loved more than his dad. He fully recognized the sacrifices and floor-pacing on his behalf. But there was a whole other side to his childhood. Valon held a lot of secret bitterness over

Ledger staying with Ry. While technically both men were his legal parents, Ry would never be anything to Valon. The pent-up anger he felt over a childhood of terror at Ry's hands was massive. It was soul-consuming. Then there was Kash. Kash had been his first love. His first everything, really. The traits Kash had that had Valon falling for him were the same traits that made Valon push him away. Valon had been forced to accept some harsh truths about himself over the years. Now he saw his issues for what they were; the things he loved the most were the same things killing him.

It should feel strange to see Kash with his dad, but something fundamental had changed inside Valon. He had become someone no one knew any longer. Just as no one recognized him, Valon barely knew anyone in his life anymore. Nonetheless, he wanted the pair to be happy. They were the only people he cared about. His dad and Kash deserved the love they had found in each other. He wanted that for them. It was just that Valon hurt for himself. Thankfully, for the last three months, Marc had distracted him. The guy was big and funny. He made Valon smile. Valon hadn't done that in a long time and meant it. Marc was his friend. For real. Valon had given up on having anyone come into his life who cared about anything other than his fame and money. People only wanted what he could do for them now financially, or just by being seen at his side. Marc was different. The way he focused on Valon, being open and genuine, had Valon relaxing his shoulders and unclenching his jaw. It was nice.

No matter his feelings about anyone, a full day with Kash and Dad always mentally exhausted him. While he had regained some genuine happiness and smiles with Marc, he still found himself keeping up an act with his family. Marc let him brood in the silence, if that was what Valon needed. At his dad's, he had to fake his way through every second any time his mood changed. There was no way he was doing this sober. As they headed out, and Valon headed for the driver's side, he pulled a laced cigar from the front pocket of his shirt.

"You said you wanted to drive today," Marc reminded him before he could climb behind the wheel. In a minute, he was about to be too high to think, and it wouldn't matter much to him. They would be fine.

Marc snatched his fun stick before Valon could even light the thing. Without a word, he walked to the passenger side of Valon's SUV and opened the door. "Get in."

Valon huffed. Marc didn't defy him on many things, but this was one. "That's coming out of your paycheck."

Marc shrugged. His jaw was set. "Do what you feel you need to do. You can have your dumbass cigar back when we get home. You're not ruining your visit with your dad."

Valon dutifully climbed into the passenger seat. "I wouldn't have ruined anything."

Marc snorted and closed the door behind him. Valon watched him circle the vehicle to the driver's side. He didn't know why he couldn't look away, but he was always like this. Valon felt like there was a revelation on the edge of his brain ready to break free. Like déjà vu or something.

Marc met his gaze the moment he settled behind the wheel. He had Hawaiian-blue eyes. They were nearly impossible to look away from sometimes. "I know you don't think you act differently when you smoke, but you do. While I'm unbothered by that, you're Ledger's kid. You can spend a couple of hours being the person he remembers." Marc held up his hand, stopping Valon before he even began. "I know you're sick of pretending to be what everyone else expects. This is different. Your dad loves you for real. Don't ruin that."

Valon's throat swelled. He kind of wanted to lash out. But Marc had said he knew Valon was sick of playacting. Valon had never admitted that to anyone. Not even Marc. He couldn't argue. No one saw him the way Marc did.

When Valon didn't argue, Marc gave him a sharp nod and backed from the driveway. They rode in silence. That was actually rare for them. Normally, they kept the radio turned down so they didn't have to talk over the noise. Now, the lack of sound was heavy on Valon's chest. He opened his phone and clicked around, hoping to distract himself. He had messages.

Unknown number: *Hey baby boy. I've been thinking about you. Please respond. You're all I have.*

Valon didn't even read the next message. He trashed everything and blocked the latest number. Valon doubly hated having his cigar taken away now. He pasted on his most charming smile.

"Ry just sent me a bunch of texts. May I please have my cigar back? Two puffs and I'll put it out."

The look Marc shot him said it all. He shouldn't have asked. "You're not messing up a day with a real father because of the shittiness of another."

Now Valon was pissed. "I've been doing that my whole fucking life. Turn around. I'll call Dad and let him know we're not coming."

Marc growled. "Stop it, Valon. Your addiction is showing."

It was the wrong thing to say. They sat at a red light. Valon got out and started walking. He knew the way. Valon wasn't a fucking child. Marc had sworn he wouldn't be this way. He had promised he knew Valon was the boss.

It didn't take long for Marc to pull over and reach him. "God fucking damn it, Valon. Here." He pulled Valon to a stop and shoved the cigar his way. He crowded Valon so no one could see him. "Take your goddamn drugs. What do I care? Just get in the fucking car before you start a riot or cause a wreck. You know you can't just burst into public like this."

Valon's throat swelled. He let Marc shuffle him back inside the vehicle. Valon didn't even notice they were back on their way. He stared down at his hand. Valon couldn't bring himself to light the stick he held. He fought back tears all the way to their destination. When the SUV stopped, Valon couldn't move. His gaze wouldn't budge from his lap and open hand. Valon hated himself the way he always did. He never did anything right.

Marc opened his door.

Valon couldn't unfreeze.

Marc's hand smoothed down Valon's arm—like stroking a cat. He took the cigar from Valon and tucked it into Valon's shirt pocket. "I'm sorry."

The lump in Valon's throat was too big for Valon to respond.

Marc stroked the palm of Valon's still-open hand. "It's okay." He sounded soothing as hell. "Breathe, beautiful. No one is angry with you. You'll always be safe with me."

A tear hit Valon's lap, making him realize how far he had spiraled. He took a breath and then another. The fear ebbed. His vision cleared. The humiliation set in.

Valon wiped his face and squared his shoulders. He grabbed the sunglasses from the visor and stepped out, forcing Marc to take a step back. He put on the glasses and left Marc to close the door. As always, he forced a smile to his lips. Life had been killing him for a long time. What did one more day matter?

Chapter Two

Valon spent the day punishing him. From the moment Marc got him back in the SUV after his tantrum, he only spoke to Marc to give him instructions for the day. All the genuine smiles were gone. Marc knew exactly where he had gone wrong. People forcing Valon to live life their way was one of the many things that had broken Valon, and Valon was a shattered mess beneath a flawless package.

He always knew the signs of a total crash out. Valon had smiled and talked, doing all the right things with Ledger and Kash. Marc felt sick the entire time. He saw beneath the mask. He recognized the need to run in Valon's eyes. Marc held his breath with a lead weight in his stomach. He would like to say it was almost a relief when Valon left, but it wasn't. This was the part where Marc always expected to be found out. He followed Valon at a safe distance, staying invisible. Marc waited until Valon was inside and then waited fifteen minutes longer. Marc was about seventy-five percent certain Valon was safe inside the private members-only club. Still, he couldn't stomach the thought of the other twenty-five percent. As he climbed out of the car, he bit back a tired sigh. The membership fees at Club Affinity were outrageous. While Marc made damn good money, he didn't like emptying his bank account just to get inside the exclusive kink club.

He nodded at the security at the door as he scanned his card. The club was actually underground. Once through the door, he had to make an immediate left to get downstairs. It was pretty rare for things to be underground in California. He understood why this place had been built the way it had. Ultimate security and privacy. No one was looking through windows here.

After a quick jog down the stairs, Marc passed the private reservation-only rooms. At the end of the hall, double doors waited, hiding the crowd of kinksters partying inside. As he pushed his way through the door, loud music washed over him. Marc used his training to stick to the shadows. That meant skirting blatant sexual acts. But Marc had his sights set on Valon and wouldn't be distracted. When he reached a spot where he had a clear view to keep watch, Marc leaned against the wall and crossed his arms, settling in.

"Guard duty again?"

Marc glanced the club owner's way. "That's what I get paid to do."

Zeus settled in beside him, helping him prop up the wall.

Marc scowled with aggravation. Zeus looked like a god. All eyes followed him every second. Marc was trying to stay hidden. Thankfully, Valon didn't seem to be interested in Zeus. He danced like no one was watching while looking completely unrecognizable.

"You know I've got him, right? Nothing will happen to him here."

Marc snorted. "I've seen the way your husband distracts you. That's not a risk I'm willing to take."

Zeus chuckled. The laugh sounded every bit as sexy as the man. Marc wasn't immune. Zeus simply didn't hold a candle to Valon, as far as Marc was concerned. No one did.

"Fair enough. But you should take into consideration how badly no one here wants to lose their membership. They absolutely would if they did anything to harm anyone here or their reputation outside this club. You read the contract."

He had. When it came to someone as famous as Valon, all it took was one picture. One whisper. The damage would be irreparable. His only saving grace was his outfit, which kept his identity pretty hidden.

"I think I'll stay, nonetheless."

Zeus nodded. "You pay your dues to be here like everyone else. I'd never suggest you leave or not protect your client. I'm only pointing out that if people recognize you, and all you do is stare at him, one night, someone will put two and two together."

Fuck. He hadn't considered that. "Well, fuck."

There was no judgment in Zeus' eyes. It was obvious he truly to only meant to help. "Maybe you should find a way to join in around here. If you only plan to watch, maybe spend some time enjoying a bit of voyeurism. People will assume that's just what you're into and ignore you."

He honestly hated that idea. Marc didn't know if that made him strange, but he wasn't a watcher. Even as the thought ran through his head, Valon mesmerized him as he danced. Arms in the air, adorable booty moving to the music. A lion's tail swung behind him, making Marc incapable of looking away. His full pajamas, hood and all, did nothing to hide him from Marc. God, he was sexy.

"I see."

Zeus' quietly spoken words had Marc looking his way. "I'm sorry. What?"

Zeus shook his head. "Have a safe night."

Marc watched Zeus move to another man hiding in the shadows. The huge, muscular, dark-haired guy screamed danger, but he smiled the moment Zeus approached. Marc's attention returned to watching the way Valon's body moved to match the music. He looked to be in his own world, dancing alone and ignoring everyone. Beautiful. Marc's whole world.

A few minutes passed. Marc didn't even notice. But his attention went on high alert when the same man Zeus had spoken with headed Valon's way. Marc straightened away from the wall. Every sense he possessed screamed danger. He watched as the behemoth ran his hand across the small of Valon's back, touching him unnecessarily to get his attention. Valon visibly stiffened. Marc took a step in their direction. Valon shook his head. The guy didn't leave. He was all smiles. Fuck.

Marc closed the distance between them and hauled Valon backward against his chest. "Is there a problem here?"

Laughing eyes met his question. "None at all." Mr. Flirtatious walked away still smiling.

Marc got the feeling the guy enjoyed Marc's reaction. With a crisis averted, the truth sank in. His clandestine guarding was at an end. There was no going back now.

The instant Valon had found himself in Marc's hold, he melted. It didn't even seem odd that he knew Marc's arms without looking. Then his persistent stranger walked away, and Valon didn't know what to do. How long had he known? Why was he here? Then, his body just moved. Valon went back to dancing, letting the music fill him with peace. He held on to Marc's arms, stopping him from getting away. It didn't take long for the peace he sought to have a different goal.

Marc felt wooden pressed against him. He kept backing the lower half of his away, stopping Valon from finding out if Marc was hard for him or not. Valon needed Marc's desire. If Marc wanted him, then he would forget he saw Valon here. He wouldn't ask questions.

Marc untangled himself. His warmth disappeared.

Valon didn't look to see where he had gone. All joy seeped from him. He looked around, taking in the place that had brought him freedom. So many people lived their true selves around him. He walked away. One more thing lost to him. He would call Zeus tomorrow and cancel his membership. As he crawled inside his car without Marc guarding his back, the hole inside him opened. He didn't know if he had simply slipped away before Marc noticed or if Marc chose to stay the invisible tail Valon hadn't noticed before tonight. Either way, it didn't matter. There was no keeping him safe from the poison inside him.

Less than two miles from the club, Valon veered off the road and parked. He lit up a laced cigar and reclined his seat. Valon smoked while he stared at the gray surface above him. He saw nothing. Valon had found a healthy way to vanish, but it seemed he wouldn't be allowed to keep that. So here he was, getting high to escape. Valon recognized how low he had gotten. He wanted to claim this was rock bottom, but he knew better. For now, he still had his music, reputation, and fans. Damned if his lowest point didn't always also have a basement. Each time he felt the flames of hell licking his skin, it turned out to be just Ry breathing too hard down his neck wanting money. No one seemed to care or notice he was slowly dying.

Everything around him swam.

A hysterical laugh escaped him.

Valon finished his cigar, ensuring his brain couldn't function. With nothing else to do, Valon rolled onto his side. He grabbed the tail of his pajamas as he curled into a ball. The material felt extra soft as he stroked it, soothing himself. One of these days, he would simply pass away from the drugs. They would find him just like this: dead in his car, hanging on to a lion's costume with no comfort but a fleece tail. The entire world would shrug when the coroner announced it was an overdose. Another rock star going out like a typical celebrity. Tears rolled from Valon's eyes, immediately carried away by his leather seats. He wondered if Marc would miss him. His dad and Kash had each other. Who did Marc have? Why hadn't he asked? Because, like always, he had been too self-absorbed. Maybe if he lived, Valon would dig into his life. It seemed like something a friend would do.

Valon's eyes closed. The cloud where he floated carried him to a dreamless sleep. Nothing penetrated the inky void the drugs had created for him. Peace at last.

Chapter Three

VALON STRETCHED AND SAVORED the soft sheets surrounding him. He burrowed deeper under the covers. Since he had nowhere to be, Valon settled in for a few more hours of sleep. The scent of pancake syrup and coffee was the first thing to pull at his senses, clearing his head. Something tickled the back of his mind. Fuck. He had gotten high again. Dumb.

Wait.

Valon shot upright. He blinked at his surroundings. Nothing looked familiar. His heart tried crawling into his throat. From the center of a full-sized bed, Valon took everything in. The walls were blank. Yet the longer he looked, the more he sensed he had seen these walls before. It was like a hazy memory trying to form before slipping away again. Everything was soft, including the unfamiliar pajamas he wore.

French toast sticks and orange juice waited on a round table that looked as if it was meant for kids. There were toys stacked in the corner, along with coloring books. Valon lost the ability to see any of that. His gaze was locked on the man sitting in a nearby rocking chair. Marc watched him in a way Valon hadn't seen before. A sense of peace washed over him. The reaction seemed like the most foolish one he could land on, but it was Marc. He was safe.

"Where am I?"

Marc didn't answer. Instead, he motioned toward the table. "Come eat while it's still warm. I know you must be starving. You barely ate anything yesterday."

"I barely eat anything any day."

Marc nodded. His expression remained completely neutral. "That's over. Eat."

Valon climbed out of bed. The pj pants he wore didn't slide down his hips, but they were nearly a foot too long for him. Valon had to fight his way across the room to keep from tripping over them. He didn't realize he twisted the hem of his t-shirt between his hands as the nervousness set in. When he noticed, he let go. Marc wasn't acting like Marc. He didn't feel quite as safe anymore.

Valon pulled the lone chair away from the tiny table. It took him a second to find a way to sit in the minuscule chair and also get close enough to the table to eat. His knees banged the edge. Marc stood and helped him, turning the chair. He got the chair closer. Marc made a plate for Valon, drowning the toast in what looked to be homemade hot syrup.

"Eat."

Valon chewed his bottom lip as he watched Marc reclaim his seat. He couldn't take it. "I guess you're probably curious about the lion costume."

"Not really."

Valon kept talking. "It's my disguise when I go to the club. If people don't know it's me, I don't need a guard."

Marc's expression remained blank. "Save your excuses. I don't want to hear it."

His voice was stern and made Valon immediately withdraw. He ate the soggy bread in front of him. His sweet Marc was gone, Valon supposed. More likely than not, he was finally done with Valon's shit. That was fair, he guessed. He still didn't understand where they were.

"Where are we?" The ice wall Valon always used to protect himself was firmly in place now. He wouldn't let Marc turning on him be the final straw that broke him.

Marc didn't respond.

Valon pushed away from the table and headed for the door. He was beholden to no one.

"I told you to eat."

Valon spun on him. "I don't like bossy people!" He yelled the words before even he knew what he planned to say. "As much as no one wants to hear me, I'm an adult. You'd think getting famous would've given me at least a hair of freedom, but no. Men like you spend their entire fucking day keeping me in line." The air quotes he used around that last bit came from his soul. He was done with this. "You know what? You're fired. It's time you found another client. I'm done with babysitters. Let the crowds tear me to pieces or what the fuck ever. I'm fucking done."

Marc softened. A small smile played on his lips. “Stop being a brat and eat your breakfast.”

Valon didn’t move.

Marc gave him puppy-dog eyes. “For me?”

Fuck him. Why couldn’t Valon tell Marc no? Valon slowly made his way back to the table. This time he knew how to adjust the chair to sit. He quietly ate. His shoulders remained tense. The food was already cold. He kept his mind on lockdown. Valon had no idea what was happening, but he actually cared deeply for Marc. No doubt he scared Marc, finding him in his car. Especially since Valon obviously hadn’t been conscious in any way for God knew how many hours. Valon got it. He terrified himself too. The wildest part, and the part Marc would no doubt think was a lie, Valon wasn't an addict. He could walk away from the drugs at any time. Valon had done it before. He didn't crave the high. Valon didn't even like getting high. He had always disliked the feeling of being out of control. The problem was he hated himself even more, and he couldn't escape that.

The sound of moaning came through the wall. "Oh. This is one of the private rooms at Affinity." There was no life in Valon's voice. The spark was gone from inside him.

Marc dipped his chin. "It's the quiet room for when members get overwhelmed."

"It's used for Littles." He didn't know why he corrected Marc. Valon couldn't find any other tone but dead.

Marc shrugged. "I suppose it's that too. Zeus said quiet room. It's his place. I didn't question him."

Valon drank his juice to placate Marc. He pushed to his feet. "Thanks for saving me or whatever. I'm going home." Valon didn't understand why Marc hadn't taken him there. Granted, Affinity was closer, but still. If he had done all this, he could've taken Valon home. Valan grabbed the doorknob and turned. Nothing happened. He checked the handle. There was no lock. He tried again. Nothing.

His eyes narrowed as his temper set in. "Let me out."

Marc kept rocking, seeming totally unbothered. "Sorry. Can't."

"Can't or won't?"

Marc's expression never changed. "Can't. Only Zeus has the key."

Valon growled. "Fine. I'll get it from him." He banged on the door, calling Zeus' name and demanding to be set free.

"This is a kink club, Val. No one out there thinks you're serious. This is a playroom. They probably think this is part of our game."

He was right, and that only served to spike his temper higher. "You did this. How could you do this to me? *Why* would you do this?"

For the first time, Marc showed his true feelings. His face distorted with rage. "*I* didn't do a goddamn thing. *You* did this to yourself. I'm fed up with watching you implode. So, guess what? You're staying right here until you tell me what in the fuck is going on with you."

Everything snapped closed inside him. He made a dismissive gesture. "I'm a rockstar, living the rockstar life. You can open the door now."

"Try again. This time, assume I'm not stupid."

A huff of pure irritation burst from Valon. "I'm a goddamn adult. You don't get to force me into anything."

Marc stood.

Valon immediately shrank. He didn't know this version of Marc. Maybe, like Ry, he was two different people. Valon wrapped his arms around himself. He felt the blood drain from his face. Maybe Marc would hurt him.

Marc froze halfway across the room. His expression changed from enraged to hurt. "Wait. Are you scared of me right now?"

Valon didn't respond. His mind had gone to a safer place. He had taught himself how to protect his sanity while someone hurt him. Maybe Marc could destroy his body, but he couldn't have Valon's soul. That would always belong to music. He sang a song inside his head while he dissociated. Maybe he should go back to writing music. That had saved him before. Writing was definitely better than the self-destructive ways Valon had used to escape. The thing was, he was too scared to think clearly enough to do anything. He was fucking terrified all hours of the day. There was no peace inside him. Below the surface, all Valon had to focus on was the fear. He thought he might be going slowly insane.

A warm palm smoothed down his back. "It's okay, beautiful. You never have anything to worry about when you're with me. You're safe."

Valon blinked. He was back in bed. This time, he wasn't alone. Marc's huge body engulfed him. His face was buried against Marc's chest. Marc whispered comforting words into Valon's hair. Well, fuck. Nothing like humiliating himself again. He could die now.

Holy shit. When Marc had decided to force Valon into facing whatever went on in his head, Marc hadn't expected this. He still didn't know what drove Valon to self-destruct, but he knew one damn thing. Someone had physically hurt Valon. He had never seen anyone cower and disappear like that. While Valon hadn't moved, he had vanished from the room just the same. He had taken his mind and fled.

Marc would like to claim he hadn't thought Valon's secrets were that bad, but he couldn't. He had known something truly ugly haunted Valon. Marc hadn't expected the absolute dissociation. Valon hadn't even returned to reality when Marc had carried him to bed. He was like a limp rag doll. It was honestly terrifying. Almost as chilling as tracking Valon's phone to an empty parking lot. Marc had thought Valon was dead inside his car. He had been in a fetal position, holding the tail of his costume. By the time Marc had finally gotten inside the car, he had been in full panic mode. Then Valon didn't wake up, no matter what Marc tried. Zeus had driven by and caught sight of him. Marc didn't know what he would have done without Zeus' help. It turned out his cousin was married to a doctor for the stars. Very discreet. Once they had been assured Valon would live, Zeus had suggested this plan. It seemed—of all crazy things—Zeus had been a deprogrammer of some sort for a spy program. He didn't go into many details, but Zeus had the knowhow to break through people's psyche. Marc desperately needed that help at the moment.

Zeus had warned him this wouldn't be easy, and that Marc likely wouldn't like what he learned. But Marc didn't have a choice any longer. Valon was one bad night away from dying from this bullshit. Marc had to know what was going on. He held Valon and tried to comfort him. Marc knew the instant Valon came back to himself. His entire body stiffened.

Valon cleared his throat, but his voice still sounded strained when he spoke. “Sorry about that. Sometimes I do that.”

Marc closed his eyes and savored a moment of holding Valon. He didn’t think he could fix a thing. “I’m the one who’s sorry. I shouldn’t have brought you here. It’s obvious you don’t think enough of me to let me help.” Marc hated the things he said, but he couldn’t stop. He was gutted that Valon thought he would hurt him. Marc rolled away and sat up. “I’ll call Zeus and tell him to let us out. It’s my fault for thinking we were friends. I get it. You’re my boss, and I’m your employee. I won’t mistake my place again.” Goddamn it. Every word he spoke hurt, but they were the truth. Marc wanted so fucking badly to be important to Valon. He wanted to be the person Valon finally turned to for help. It seemed he was set on drowning, and there wasn't a damn thing Marc could do about it. He moved to stand.

Valon snagged the back of his shirt and held on. They sat frozen in silence until Valon finally spoke. "You're my friend." His voice sounded so small and hurt that Marc thought his chest would cave. "I'd actually—if you're okay with it—I think I'd like to be held a little longer."

Well, fuck. He didn't have to ask Marc twice. Marc turned and settled back in, tucking Valon against his chest. Without thought, his lips found Valon's forehead. He couldn't stop the light kiss he placed there. Marc didn't speak. His throat was too tight. Valon had called him a friend. Considering he was sickeningly in love with the guy, Marc would take it. Valon Stark was willingly in his arms. Wow. All his obsessions raced to the surface and crippled him. No one could or would ever know how Marc had dreamed and plotted.

Valon brushed his fingertips across Marc's clavicle, petting him. "More times than I can count, I've come to your room at night and stood outside your door." Marc's entire existence held on to Valon's every word. "I knew I could knock, and you'd let me in. You'd keep me safe. Maybe it would mean just sleeping like this so I can actually freaking sleep." His voice got stronger the more he spoke. "But then I'd go back to bed and fall apart until I'd finally light up and drift away."

"You should've knocked."

He felt Valon shake his head. "You're the only person who knows me who doesn't think I'm a horrible person. If you knew anything about me, you'd look at me differently. That would break my heart."

Marc needed Valon to keep talking. "There's nothing you can say to me that would make me see you in a negative light. As wild as it may sound, you're my best friend, even if I'm not yours."

Valon stroked him again but didn't respond right away. "I'm so used to keeping everything inside, protecting other people's happiness, I don't know how to open myself. But I know there's an ugliness in me I can't burden anyone else with."

"I want to carry it with you. Just start somewhere. Open your mouth and let the ugliness go. I'm begging you to stop killing yourself while I'm right here, wanting the job of being your peace."

He felt Valon take a deep breath. "Dad and Kash don't understand. Maybe you won't either. I couldn't get away from them fast enough when I hit it big."

That one threw Marc for a loop. "Is that because of them falling in love or whatever?"

A humorless laugh rumbled from Valon. "If I'd let him, Kash would've stayed with me forever. So, no. It had nothing, yet everything, to do with them." Valon took another breath that sounded hard-fought. "It was Ry."

Valon's earlier reaction and his confession had a terrible sense of foreboding building in Marc.

Thankfully, Valon kept talking so Marc didn't have to demand an explanation.

"I don't know why he hated me. Maybe that's not true. I think he saw me as the reason he was stuck in a marriage he didn't want. Hell, maybe I took too much attention away from him. No matter the reason, he took every opportunity to torture me in the worst ways. Then he threatened me if I told anyone, he would kill Dad and Kash. Ry said that so often that—sometimes—I would be with them and feel like I was suffocating. Maybe I even came to hate them a little for trapping me in hell. Then I won the lottery of musical dreams. I ran fast and hard. Even though I'd never tell them, I had no plans to talk to either of them again. I'd gotten my escape. Of course, no one let me leave them, and the distance created some huge guilt over punishing Dad for Ry. But there's still a small part of me that wonders how in the hell no one saw me suffering. Then I remind myself I can be a damn good actor when I want."

Marc felt Valon hesitating. He knew there was more. Marc couldn't let him stop now. "What about Ry?"

The ugly laugh that escaped Valon made chills run down his spine. "He showed up the second he thought I had anything he could take. When I gleefully shut him down, he hired people to try to rough me up and intimidate me into basically handing him the reins to my financials. I kept hiring guards to protect me, except none of them seemed to understand how dangerous Ry is. Maybe they even thought I should be helping out my legal parent."

Marc drew a sharp breath as the rage built.

Unfortunately, Valon wasn't finished. "Then, one night after a concert, I went out partying with the band. I got shit-faced and let a guy lure me to an alley-way behind the club. When he attacked, I didn't see it coming. Of course, I'd shooed away security so I could play. So I was stuck and fighting for my life. I don't know exactly how it happened. One second, I was on the ground, scrambling to get away. The next, I had a broken beer bottle in my hand that I had stabbed into the guy's throat."

Marc kind of wanted to tell Valon to stop. He didn't need the rest. Anything more, and he would kill Ry.

"I just kind of froze. He was choking on his own blood, and all I could think about was how this mess could ruin my career. I'd be forced back into a life I can't stomach. Then he was dead, and I didn't know what to do. I called Bond. He's been my manager since day one. I didn't know how he would handle it, but I knew he would. In minutes he was there, whisking me away and telling me not to worry about a thing. He would make sure no one ever knew what happened."

Valon shivered, and Marc held him tighter. The horrific story continued.

"My guards were furious I had disappeared. There was a lot of screaming. They quit, and I ended up labeled a problem client. A title I made worse when I started having the feeling again—like no one was even trying to protect me. The one thing I didn't consider, though, was Ry. He knew he had sent that guy. Ry knew that guy went missing afterward. That's when the blackmail began."

Each time Marc thought he had reached the pinnacle of his anger, Valon added another log to the fire. Marc squeezed his eyes shut. Valon needed him calm. He got the feeling he was the only person ever to hear this story. Marc understood so much now, though. The way Valon treated Ledger and Kash. How Valon acted when it came to security. Marc saw it all now. Valon was trapped in a nightmare, and no one helped. Still, Valon had gone to his dad and shown him affection. He had smiled and cheered as Kash married his dad. The hurt and fear Valon choked down every second was enough to kill anyone. But now Marc knew, and Valon wasn't who would lose their life over this.

Marc kissed Valon's forehead again. "You have me now. It's time for you to close your eyes and sleep without fear, okay? Nothing else will happen to you. That's a promise I can keep."

He felt Valon nod and relax. Despite just waking up, Valon was out like a light in minutes. Life had drained the fuck out of him. Marc would fix everything.

Chapter Four

With Valon safely hanging out with his dad and Kash for the day, Marc headed for the home office. Steel Security Services had been his career for the past seven years. He had gone from working venues and minor jobs to slowly working his way into full-time live-in security. It wasn't a life meant for everyone. A live-in bodyguard for a celebrity was the highest-paying job a Steel employee could achieve. All it took was the right combination of chemistry and level of fame to set up guards for life. It was a tradeoff, though. He lived on Valon's schedule. It had taken him a few days to find the time to run this errand.

The stone building that housed the main office of Steel Security was conveniently located in one of the poshest parts of Los Angeles. Part of their success was simply them being centered where the richest people saw their sign every day. The rest was reputation. Steel provided the best, making him the top choice for celebrities. There were locations around the country in the most popular places for the rich and famous clientele. Each time Marc walked through the door, he felt his posture change. He walked taller with squared shoulders. Marc was proud of his job. He hadn't expected to be more than a handyman of some sort. While a lot of those jobs could pay pretty damn well, the thought of Marc having to live that way day after day made him want to step into traffic. Not every job was for everyone. He was damn grateful he landed this one.

The minute Marc stepped into sight of Steel's office. Steel came to his feet and circled his desk. "What's wrong?"

That was a fair question, considering how rarely he came here.

There was a line between Steel's brows. His eyes, which matched his name, were filled with concern. "You're not quitting, are you? No one else here can handle Valon."

That should have chafed. Valon deserved better. But he had no intention of disabusing Steel of that notion. Marc had to be irreplaceable in Valon's life.

"No, it's nothing like that, but I'd appreciate it if we could speak in private."

Steel motioned toward the front desk. "Hold my calls."

Marc followed on Steel's heels. Steel was a solid country boy. He had broad shoulders from years of hard work. A hint of gray tinted his dark hair. He was also an extremely likable guy. But when it came to keeping people safe, he was not a man to be messed with. Marc needed that side of him now.

The moment they were in Steel's office, Marc closed the door behind him. He took the seat across from Steel at his desk. Marc didn't waste time. "Valon is being blackmailed."

Steel didn't even flinch. In their business, these things weren't uncommon. Plus, Steel was all about solutions. "Do we know who it is?"

Marc dipped his chin. "His estranged father, Ry Kenway. He's..."

"I know him," Steel said, saving Marc a long-winded story about Valon's parents' split. "He's a bastard."

Marc nodded. "Agreed. He's ruining Valon's life. This comes after he spent Valon's entire childhood torturing him."

Steel's eyebrows snapped together. His face hardened. "He was abused." It wasn't a question. It sounded more like Steel needed to say the words aloud.

Marc's hands rose and fell, showing he had nothing. "I don't know what to do, but this can't continue. Valon won't last much longer. The strain is killing him."

Steel nodded. His gaze seemed to turn inward. He snapped back to life and grabbed his phone. After finding whatever contact he sought, Steel set the phone on the desk and left it on speaker. The sound of ringing filled the air.

"Good morning. Steel Security Services. This is Clover."

Despite everything, Marc smiled at the sound of Clover's voice. He was the receptionist at the Washington office. Marc said "receptionist" loosely. He ran the show at his location.

"Hey, Clover. It's Steel."

An adorable squeal came through the phone's speaker. "I haven't talked to you in so long. How are you?"

A small smile played on Steel's lips. Everyone who met Clover was immediately smitten. He was too nice to dislike. "I'm good, but I need to ask a favor."

Clover didn't hesitate. "Of course. Anything."

"I have a client who's being harassed and blackmailed."

Clover gasped. "That's awful."

Steel nodded as if Clover could see him. "It is. Not to mention, this is a huge client of ours. He's also my cousin's step-kid."

Marc hadn't thought about that. Of course, Steel would know about Ry.

“Tell me what you need. I’m here to help.”

“I’d like to have all of his calls except for an approved list re-routed to you.”

“Ooh. The confuse and aggravate method.”

A huge smile exploded across Steel’s face. “Exactly. I’ll warn you, it’s our client’s legal parent, so he'll definitely pull that card on you.”

“That’s horrible.” Clover sounded genuinely horrified. “Well, just leave it to me. He’ll never get past me.”

Steel’s smile never dimmed. “I know. You’re the best.”

“Awww, ditto.”

Steel's smile softened. "I'll send you the full details and get everything set up. Thank you for this. You'll see it come bonus time."

"You're too good to me." The sweet note in Clover's voice warmed even Marc's heart.

"I'll talk to you later."

Clover perked up even more. "Okay. It was good to hear your voice."

"You too. Bye." Steel disconnected the call and focused on Marc. "That'll take care of any phone calls. He has you by his side. That's two things. I'd also like to bring in a property guard, making it impossible for Ry to get to him while he's at home. Blackmailers never actually release anything. Ruining Valon would ensure he never saw another dime. But this definitely buys us time to find a way to turn the tables."

Marc nodded along. He appreciated Steel hadn't asked what Ry had on Valon. "This all sounds great. I knew you'd know how to approach things."

Steel leaned back in his chair, making the huge leather piece look small. He eyed Marc. For a moment, Marc expected Steel to lecture him about being too close to his client. "You're good for Valon. I'm not sure any other guard would've found this out."

Marc slowly nodded, trying to find the right words. "He really isn't difficult. I think he's just tired of being under everyone's microscope. Imagine not even being able to relax at home because everyone thinks you're too wild to give a moment's peace. People never stop watching your every move. I think I would've snapped under the pressure a long time ago."

Steel sat forward. "Makes sense. Keep me in the loop. We'll find a way to stop this. In the meantime, we can keep Ry chasing his tail and give Valon time to breathe."

Marc stood. "Thank you. I'll let you get back to work. It's almost time for me to pick up Valon from his dad's place."

"Have you talked to Kash about this?"

Marc shook his head. "I don't know why, but it didn't feel like a good idea."

Steel made a dismissive gesture. "It's fine. Leave it to me. Kash is definitely someone to manage carefully."

Marc wasn't surprised. While Kash could be a huge goofball, Marc had always seen a darkness in Kash. If Marc told Kash what he had learned, Kash would kill Ry. Marc wanted that pleasure.

In unison, Valon and Ledger set the two-person outdoor swing in motion. Leaned back, enjoying the perfect weather, everything felt calmer than he could recall in a long time. Before Kash had married his dad, he had forced Valon to lean on his dad even though he had no idea what was going on with Valon. Valon was grateful for that now. Ledger had always been the best dad. Valon knew if Ledger had known Ry had harmed him in any way, he probably would have killed the guy. That was the thing, though. Valon hadn't wanted to lose his dad to prison. Powering through seemed to be the best choice. Too many things to name had left him bitter. Bitterness had moved to loneliness. He wanted to let it go. Ry wouldn't let him. But Valon wasn't dumb. He knew nothing had ever stood between him and safety except himself. Still, he didn't know if it mattered any longer. The past was the past.

"If I ask you a question, will you answer me honestly?"

Valon was so in his head, the question caught him off guard. A nervous chuckle escaped him. "I can try."

Ledger didn't look his way. He gave a sharp nod. "Are you an addict?"

The question surprised a bark of laughter from Valon. "No, Dad. I'm not an addict."

"Did Ry ever touch you inappropriately?"

Valon had still been laughing when the question hit, sounding like Ledger ripped off a bandage. If he hadn't been so caught off guard, Valon might have answered differently. "No. He just tortured me and beat the shit out of me every time you weren't watching." Even Valon was surprised by his response.

Ledger's eyes closed as if his worst fears had been recognized. His throat worked as he swallowed before looking Valon's way. The pain in his eyes made Valon want to run. This was why he hadn't said anything.

Valon scrambled to make the hurt disappear. He couldn't take it. Valon kept his voice light and playful. "It's cool, Dad. Forget I said anything. I'm an adult. It's in the past. It's my fault, really. I could've said something back then."

"Don't do that."

Valon's lungs tried to seize at Ledger's words.

Ledger didn't stop there. "You're not okay. I can see how hard you're trying, but I can also see the desperation in your eyes each time you're here. You can't wait to get away."

It seemed there was no avoiding this. "Please stop. I love you. You're my dad."

"And I failed you." Ledger's voice cracked as he said the words.

Valon's eyes burned. He couldn't do this. It hurt too much. "I should go."

Ledger looked defeated. There were tears in his eyes. "Damn, Valon. Don't run away again. My heart breaks every time you can't get away from me fast enough. Did Kash know?"

It seemed that as long as Ledger kept asking questions, he would answer. "No one knew. I'm a pretty good actor when I try. You were happy. I couldn't be the reason you two got divorced. Plus, what if you hadn't believed me? Ry was damn good at making you think everyone else was the liars or you were being paranoid." The more Valon spoke, the more he realized how true every word was. His hands lifted and fell to his lap. "I love you. You're an amazing dad. Always have been. I'm the one who was too paralyzed with fear to say anything. There's nothing you could've done differently to change that. I know that. Even if you had left him, I never would've found the strength to tell you." He knew that because he hadn't before now. Before Marc forced his way in, and shored up his backbone. In the fervor of his speech, Valon had sat forward and turned toward Ledger. Fresh, free air filled his lungs. Valon sat back and scooted closer, snuggling beneath his dad's arm. That was where he had always felt safest. “For my own sanity, I need to leave the past behind.”

Ledger sniffed like he still fought tears, but he kissed Valon’s temple. “We should start a family game night once a month. You bring Marc, and we can take turns deciding what we play.”

Despite everything, a genuine smile exploded across Valon’s face. “I love that you’re including Marc in our family.”

They set the swing back in motion. “That’s because he is. I can see how much he cares about you. He seems like he’s a genuine friend. Your smile is real when he’s around.”

The claim danced inside his brain. Memories flowed freely. Marc did everything for him... he was everything to him. “Yeah. He’s a good person.” Valon didn’t know how else to respond. He couldn't admit his true feelings. Every day, Marc got a little deeper into his heart. Valon wanted more than his friendship. Marc didn't see him in that way. He was the one thing Valon couldn't buy. A hint of the devil spurred him. He couldn't buy Marc, but he could damn sure spoil him. A wicked laugh rose in his chest. Valon swallowed it. He could already feel Marc's passive resistance. Valon couldn't wait to get started.

Chapter Five

Marc dragged his feet through their third store of things he couldn't afford while Valon chatted and smiled. That was what kept him going. Valon looked genuinely happy today. He seemed different. Lighter. Marc couldn't wait for Valon to realize Ry didn't call anymore. He knew at some point there would be some blowback on that one. It was only a matter of time before Ry popped up like a bad penny. Marc would have to do something to keep that from happening. Unfortunately, it would take time. He didn't know how long Ry would give him. Marc needed to find out how often Ry demanded money and whatnot. But Valon was actually happy, and Marc couldn't ruin the smiles.

"Okay. This is perfect." Valon held up an expensive T-shirt that tried to look cheap, and a leather jacket made to look worn. "This is you. I wonder if this jacket would fit your broad shoulders. I might need to get one custom-made. Honestly, that's probably what I should do anyway. Custom-made clothes always fit best."

"Oh god. Please don't. That's so much money. I don't need any of this."

"Hush." Valon didn't look his way as he combed through the jeans. "This brings me joy."

Marc couldn't stop arguing. "I never want you to think I want your money." Even Marc heard the power behind his statement. Even if Valon didn't have a penny, Marc still couldn't stay away. It was Valon he wanted.

Valon stopped and met his stare. "I've been in this game long enough to know how to spot the money grabbers and clout chasers. You're neither of those things." He went back to sorting through clothes. "In fact, today, Dad said you were family. He's right. You are."

Marc's throat swelled tight and fast. He couldn't respond.

Valon turned, holding an armful of clothes. "You should try these on."

Marc let himself get dragged to the fitting rooms. He knew Valon would do what he wanted, and Marc needed to play along.

Valon shoved the clothes toward him and pushed him inside a room. "You'll look great. Trust me." He pulled the curtain closed, leaving Marc no other choice than to strip.

He felt dumb as fuck in the outrageously priced clothing. Marc knew the items had to be astronomical. They were in a store where only the richest people made it past the front door without getting turned away by security. Nothing had a price tag. If a person had to ask, they couldn't afford it.

Marc dutifully tried on the first outfit while Valon tossed more clothes over the curtain. He looked at himself in the mirror. The outfit was definitely in line with the cool upper class.

"I look dumb as hell." The defeat in his voice couldn't be masked.

"I seriously doubt that. You're not capable of looking dumb."

"Well, I do." He didn't know what it was about the entire getup, but it wasn't him. Marc looked like he played a part he had no business playing.

"Okay. Look alive. I'm coming in."

Luckily, the room was big enough for two and the ridiculous amount of clothes Valon had waiting for him.

Valon looked him up and down, openly judging the outfit. “It’s the shirt. Here.” Valon turned. He picked through the shirts until he found another. “Take that one off and try this one.”

It was a Hawaiian blue button-down. He pulled the t-shirt up and over his head and accepted the new shirt. Marc stuck his arms through the holes while Valon watched. His gaze followed Marc’s every move. The stare was unsettling. He didn’t feel like a friend was watching him. There was something different in Valon’s eyes. Marc couldn’t put a name to the emotions he saw.

Valon blew out a slow whistle. “This is it. This is the one. That shirt perfectly matches your eyes.”

Marc glanced toward the mirror. Damn. He did look good.

Valon closed the distance between them and played with the collar.

Their gazes met and held. Heat built between them. Marc didn't think he felt only what he wanted to feel. The tension was cloying. He was scared to move. Marc couldn't ruin what they had. As much as he wanted more, he wasn't unhappy with what he had. Their relationship was more than he ever dreamed could be his. Damned if Valon didn't look like he wanted to be kissed. His eyes hooded, and it was like a magnet drew them closer. Marc felt himself sway.

"Do you have everything you need in there? Can I get you some wine?"

The spell broke. Valon turned away. “Yeah. A couple of glasses of wine sounds great.”

The disappointment nearly took his knees out. Marc knew he would spend the rest of his life replaying the moment and questioning every detail. It was possible he read too much into things. That was what he had to tell himself. Anything else would crush him when it turned out the moment wasn’t real.

“I’ll go look for something different now that I've got a bead on your style.”

Marc slowly nodded even though Valon didn’t look back. He had been rendered mute. Marc was frozen solid until a cheery voice broke through his shock.

“I’ve got your wine.”

Marc tugged back the curtain.

A tall brunette in heels that made her eye level with him held an open bottle and two glasses. "Thanks." His gruff tone was out of his control.

Despite his tone, she smiled and handed over the alcohol. "No problem. Let me know if you need anything else."

Marc dipped his chin. The moment she was out of sight, he turned the bottle up, chugging half. He needed fortification if he hoped to survive the night. Hell, this shopping trip might see him dead.

Valon poured on the charm as he internally panicked. If they hadn't been interrupted earlier, he might have really kissed Marc. Marc hadn't seemed opposed. Valon had no clue what he was doing. He knew what he wanted, but—as always—he couldn't get a read on Marc. The guy was way too good at hiding his feelings. He was still waters.

They picked up dinner on the way home with their haul in tow. Marc never stopped looking horrified, but he had stopped protesting. He knew Valon. Valon didn't ask for permission. They talked all through dinner before making their way outside to sit by the pool. Valon never tired of the sound of Marc's voice. He had to keep asking questions to keep him talking.

"What was your childhood like?"

Marc's smile never dimmed. Valon wished he felt that way about his childhood. "Pretty typical, I suppose. My parents signed me up for every sport every year. I know they hoped to keep me out of trouble, but I still found ways to stir up shit. Everyone has a point in life where they have to rebel. It's like wresting control from parents. Those moments that give you what you need to strike out on your own."

Valon chuckled. "Not me. The closest thing to rebelling was bringing Kash home. He was definitely from the other side of the tracks. I expected Dad to take one look at him and refuse to let me see him again. Instead, Dad was Dad. He pulled Kash aside and peppered him with questions. From that moment on, Kash was part of the family."

"Even with Ry?"

Valon snorted. "Maybe especially with Ry. He wanted to fuck him. Really, though, that's nearly everyone's first reaction to Kash."

Marc pulled a face. "That was *not* my first reaction to meeting Kash."

"What was, then?"

Marc shook his head. "I thought, 'This guy looks like he's killed a few people.'"

Valon shrugged. "He probably has."

Marc had been leaning back in the lounge chair next to Valon. He turned sideways and sat forward, bracing his elbows on his knees. Marc looked fully invested. "Are you really okay with your dad being married to Kash? No weird feelings at all?"

Valon turned sideways to face him. Their knees brushed. He spent a moment musing over Marc's question before responding. "In a way, Kash has always been a second dad to me. Even as a teen, Kash was incredibly steady. He always guided me in the right direction, pushing me to be better." Valon paused and waved his hand wildly. "Don't get me wrong. I was in lust for sure. But I don't know. One day, I saw Dad and Kash exchange a look of exasperation over something I'd done, and I thought, 'Yeah. That tracks.' I was too immature for Kash. Kash was way too grown-up for me. He had raised himself and was more adult than he had ever been a child. Kash fits better with Dad. I can't say that realization didn't break my heart. That was more ego and pride. But I was already plotting my escape by then. My whole attitude changed to let them have each other." A self-deprecating smile pulled at his lips. "Then I got older and life got a hell of lot harder. I thought this career would be all sex, drugs, and rock'n roll. Instead, it's a stressful mess that eats your soul. I've done all the things with professionalism and maturity. I've taken my job seriously." His hands rose and fell.

"This career has been a huge blessing to me in a lot of ways. I mean, I fucking love to sing and play guitar. How many people really make it the way I have? But there're two sides to every coin." Valon couldn't look away from holding Marc's gaze. Even in the low lighting, his eyes were arresting. "This gig has also been a nightmare I can't escape at times. When I first fully realized I'd never have a normal life, it was a bit of a knife to my heart. I'll never go to the store alone or do anything in peace, really. For the rest of my life, I'll be on display. That's a crazy thing, man. It never stops being surreal. But back to the topic, and like I've told everyone before, one night, everything just hit me. Dad deserved better than me.

I'd shut him out and couldn't find my way back. Then I thought about the way I caught Dad and Kash looking at each other sometimes. They had something I never had with Kash, and they fought it because they love me. I just want them to be happy. Even if that dreamy life doesn't include me." A wry smile crossed his lips. "Especially without me."

Marc set his hands on Valon's knees and lightly squeezed. He didn't move away. It was as if he tried to physically keep Valon from running away. His voice turned serious in a way Valon rarely heard. "Did you plan to kill yourself once you had them settled?"

Valon nearly cringed at the question, but it was Marc. He didn't know how to lie to Marc. "Not directly, no. But I knew it wouldn't be long before the drugs I use to escape would end me. I knew the day would come when someone would find me in an unfortunate position where I went to sleep and never woke up. While I didn't plan to rush that along, I saw the end in sight." Valon licked his bottom lip nervously. "Except, you showed up and pulled me from the edge—mostly. That outcome doesn't feel as inevitable any longer."

Marc's expression never changed. Nothing about him screamed judgmental. Instead, he just looked like he cared. They stared at each other in silence. Something grew inside Valon's chest.

"Why are you named Valon?"

A laugh burst from Valon at the unexpected question. "It's short for Avalon."

A huge grin split Marc's face. "So every time I call you Val, I'm shortening a name that's already been shortened. Why haven't you stopped me? I love that you're named after a magical island. So fitting."

Valon shrugged. "Why would I stop you? Any time you call me Val, I know you're seeing me as more than a client."

If it were possible for Marc to look more intense, he might have scared Valon. As it was, Valon was on the edge of his seat, waiting for Marc's next move. He became hyperaware of Marc's hands on his knees. Valon swore he felt them move an inch higher.

"A new property guard has arrived."

Valon wanted to scream at another interruption.

Marc looked in the butler's direction. "I'll be there in a second."

Maybe it was for the best. It was possible these constant interferences were a sign they weren't meant to be. Maybe this was another huge mistake. He didn't want to lose his friend.

"I have to take care of this."

Valon nodded. The motion felt strange. He imagined it looked even odder.

Marc moved to stand, except he shot forward. Their mouths clashed. Valon automatically opened to accept a deeper kiss. He lost all sense. His hands moved to cup Marc's face, hoping he wouldn't slip away. He was dazed as fuck when Marc's mouth disappeared.

"If you want to act like this never happened, then I'd much rather you do that than ever stop being my friend. You mean too much to me to lose you. That would kill me, but I had to know."

"Know what?" Valon sounded every bit as disoriented as he felt.

"If you'd shove me away."

Marc fully straightened and walked away.

Valon stared at nothing while lost in everything. Their kiss had been everything he needed and more. Now, he didn't know what to do.

Marc's thoughts flew in every direction as he stepped inside. He hadn't planned that. Marc couldn't say what happened. Valon had just stared at him in a way that stole Marc's breath and good sense. He looked at Marc like Marc imagined he would while they made love. Marc couldn't shake the image in his head.

As Marc made his way to the foyer, a smile exploded across his face. When Steel had suggested sending a property guard, Marc hadn't known it would be German.

His light blue eyes focused on Marc. A smile stretched across his face. His brown hair was a mess, meaning he likely had brought his motorcycle. He held his hand out to Marc. "Hey." The moment Marc shook his hand, German pulled him into a hug and landed a solid tap on Marc's back.

Marc pulled away, smiling. "When Steel said he was sending someone, I hadn't thought it'd be you. I thought you were guarding some huge basketball star." German had been the person who trained Marc when he first started. They had worked side by side for two years. Since they were too much alike, their friendship had been inevitable.

German shrugged. "Yeah. Jathan decided to retire. He's living way out in the country on a ranch now. I was pretty useless there at the end. We decided together he likely doesn't need me anymore. Plus, he married an ex-employee of Steel's, so he's in good hands."

Marc nodded along. "Makes sense to me." He took a quick glance around to make sure no staff members were nearby. "Did Steel explain everything that's going on here?"

German nodded, turning deadly-looking, exactly how Marc needed him. "This is some bullshit, man. I tell you, the moment people get an ounce of fame or money, out comes every shitty family member they've ever had. But I've got your back now. We'll make sure Mr. Stark is safe."

Marc automatically smiled at hearing Valon's name. "Thank you. Valon is tired. This entire thing has broken him down. He's getting ready to record a new album, and the strain has kept him so on edge, his music is suffering."

German nodded along. "We've got this. I'd like to walk the property so I can check for weaknesses and start on a game plan."

Marc motioned toward the door. "After you."

German headed out with Marc. Side by side, they walked the perimeter.

Marc showed him the guard shack. He motioned toward Hank, one of the night guards who ran the front gate. "This is Hank. I'm sure you two met on your way in. He's part of the crew that vets visitors and runs the gate. Hank, this is German. He'll be patrolling the property and manning the security monitors inside."

They shook hands and exchanged nice to meet yous. From there, Marc took German along the path that led to a secret driveway where they left the property when they wanted to be unnoticed.

"There's a hidden driveway back here. It's obscured from every angle by trees and methodical design. This is typically how we leave and enter the property. Valon wants a peaceful life. He's not really one to seek attention." Marc motioned toward the pool house that—along with landscaping—did a good job of concealing the pool from sight. "That's the pool house. We spend a lot of time sitting by the water. There's a rock formation waterfall that recycles the water. The sounds relax him. For the most part, when he's not on tour, he leads a quiet life. So, honestly, he's a pretty easy client."

German chuckled. "That's the complete opposite of every description I've ever heard about being anywhere near Valon. He's run through a lot of guards who never want to see his face again. I can't tell you how many of the guys called when they heard this was my new assignment. They had a lot of horror stories."

Marc scoffed. "Not a damn one of them tried modifying their approach. They all treated Valon like he was a naughty child or something. He's a person. Valon wants the same things out of life anyone does at his age. Everyone before me tried controlling him rather than finding a way to keep him safe while he still gets to live.

He's actually pretty great. No one wanted to see beyond the rock star. I didn't make that mistake."

German's head moved in every direction, obviously making a mental map. "You sound fiercely protective of more than his physical safety. Honestly, it sounds like you care a lot about him."

Marc wouldn't pussyfoot around and try to make German think things were strictly business. "I do. We spend a lot of time alone together. Things would be awkward if we didn't talk. Once you get to know him, you'll be proud to keep him safe. He's a good person."

German blew out a sigh. "Well, that's a bit of relief to know. I'll try to follow your advice. Where will I be bunking?"

Marc changed direction and headed for the house. “I’m putting you on the opposite end of the house from Valon and me. That way, security is spread out a little. I let Valon’s butler, Nathaniel, know you were coming. He made sure your room was fully stocked with everything you need. You probably met him when you got here. He’s the person who really runs the house, so if you need anything, he’s the one to ask.” Marc would have thought giving instructions to the person who trained him would feel awkward. But it was his job to protect Valon, and it was a position he took seriously.

“Does Nathaniel go by Nathan?”

A bark of laughter burst from Marc. “I wouldn’t recommend calling him that. He takes pride in his job and in being proper. Apparently, he’s living his dream position. I didn't realize before meeting him that there's an entire sector of people whose life goal is to be butlers. It takes all kinds, I suppose."

German smiled. "I'll remember that." He looked thoughtful for a moment. "Yeah, I guess I can see his point. He's running the household of an extremely famous celebrity. In his field, that's probably the ultimate dream come true."

Marc nodded along. "Makes sense. I mean, this is my fantasy life."

As Marc made the claim, he realized that wasn't the full truth. Owning Valon's heart was the crowning pie in the sky dream. That utopia actually had started to feel like it could come true. Now that Marc finally saw a sliver of hope, he would risk it all. The worst thing that could happen was him losing access to Valon. If that ever happened, he would make Ry's stalking look like kid's stuff. Valon wouldn't get away from him.

Chapter Six

WATER DRIPPED FROM VALON'S hair before rolling down his body for the towel around his waist to absorb. His silver curls were a mixture of sticking to his shoulders and already curling wildly. Valon always tried to avoid his reflection. He didn't need to see the dark circles beneath his eyes or how overly cut his face had become from never eating.

Without permission from his brain, Valon's chin lifted. His reflection caught and held his attention. For once, Valon didn't look sleep-deprived. His silver hair needed a touch-up. Dark roots were showing. He still had the abs he had fought hard to keep. Looks mattered in this business. No matter what anyone said, a good body sold concert tickets. But he didn't look quite as skinny as he had a month ago. He hadn't realized how often he ate now just because Marc was there eating next to him. One thing Marc had was a huge appetite. Valon smiled just thinking about it. He didn't know when the clouds had parted, letting a little sunshine back into his life. Valon liked the feeling, though. He missed having the excitement of not being able to wait to see what happened next. He wanted to look forward to tomorrow again.

A soft knock landed on his bedroom door. People didn't just randomly disturb him at home. He didn't hesitate to respond.

"Come."

Marc poked his head in the door, looking unsure of his welcome. He was adorable. Valon's stomach fluttered.

"Hey. I just wanted to let you know I have the new guard settled."

Valon motioned for Marc to come inside. "There's no reason to hide behind the door. What's the new guy's name?"

Marc stepped inside the room and closed the door behind him. "It's German. He's actually who trained me when I started. I think you'll like him. He's damn good at his job."

Valon nodded. “Okay. I trust you.”

They stared at each other. It seemed like they should say something. That kiss had been amazing. Valon really wanted to do it again. He wasn’t so sure Marc felt the same. Except, Marc’s gaze swept down Valon’s body. His expression gave nothing away, but his eyes burned with lust. Someone had to make a move, deciding the fate of this growing thing. They needed either to back away now or to stop dancing.

“I didn’t shove you away.” The words were barely a whisper, but they had Marc across the room in an instant. This time, Marc’s kiss was hungry. He kissed like he had been starving for Valon’s mouth.

Valon’s towel disappeared as Marc took him down on the bed. Every place Marc touched lit him up like a firecracker. Oddly, despite being nude beneath him, Marc made no move to go beyond kissing. Meanwhile, Valon thought he might fly into a million pieces if Marc didn't give him some type of relief. Marc moved to Valon's neck, freeing Valon's mouth.

"This is the part where you lose some clothes." A nervous chuckle followed the claim. Valon couldn't stop the uncomfortable sound.

"This is farther than I ever thought you'd let me go. I don't know where to start."

Marc's awkward-sounding claim had Valon smiling hard. It was so like Marc to kiss all night, depriving himself, just because he didn't want to do anything Valon might not want. But that was the greatest thing about Marc; he made Valon brave.

"Take off your shirt."

While still straddling Valon's body, Marc sat back on his heels and peeled off his shirt. Damn. There was just so much real estate. He was real. Marc wasn't a fake Hollywood type. He was beautiful in his genuineness. Valon had to see more. He reached for the button on Marc's jeans.

Marc set his hand on Valon's stopping him. "If I lose my pants, I might lose the tiny amount of control I have. You're too sexy to be with someone like me."

Valon held his stare until Marc's hand fell away. His gaze didn't budge as he unbuttoned and unzipped Marc's jeans. Valon couldn't imagine how intense he looked because the fierceness he felt was all-consuming. No one had ever made him feel as powerful as Marc did. Even before a single look had passed between them, Marc had still treated Valon like the sun rose and fell in Valon's name. He treated Valon as if he could do no wrong, and Valon needed that like no one else understood. Valon had felt powerless his entire life. With Marc, it was as if he held all the cards, and Marc was along for the ride. Maybe that was what people really meant by ride or die. He was Valon's one and only real friend. Now he would be Valon's lover too. All Valon could do was pray he didn't fuck this up the way he did everything else. At that thought, a bit of Valon's courage drained away. He swore they shored up each other's weaknesses. The moment he stopped believing in himself, Marc took the reins.

"I've got this." Marc rolled to the side and onto his back. He pushed his jeans down his hips while Valon watched. The lust was thick when Marc's erection sprang free. Valon wanted every inch. Valon's patience disappeared. He dove for the bedside table, coming back with a condom and lube. Marc didn't argue when Valon straddled his huge body. Damn. Everything about him was delicious.

Valon rolled a condom down Marc's length. It almost wasn't wide enough. "I hope you're good with this. Being a top has never been my thing."

Marc already breathed like he had run a marathon. It was sexy as hell seeing how badly he wanted Valon. "There're no wrong answers here. I'll do anything you want."

Fuck, he really would. It was there in his eyes. "Good. There's a lot I want to do with you." Valon wasted no time lubing the outside of the condom. He would probably regret the serious lack of prep. Right then, Valon wanted the entire experience. Still, as he lowered himself onto Marc's cock, he wasn't sure he could take it. The frustration set in, and Valon was split between his need to fuck and backing away from the pain.

Unexpectedly, Marc rolled, pinning Valon beneath him. Their tongues fought while Marc fingered him. It didn't take long for Valon to want to beg. His desire was overwhelming. Marc made him feel things no one else made him feel. Between that and the way he kept Valon fully turned on, Valon was a complete mess.

"Holy shit. Please."

Something much larger replaced Marc's fingers. This time, things went smoother. He eased his way inside, going an inch at a time and backing off when needed. Marc's body was covered in a sheen of sweat by the time he was fully seated. His marathon breathing turned shaky-sounding. There was no doubt Marc hung on by a thread.

"It's okay. I want to see you come unglued and know it's me who makes you that way."

With permission given, Marc rocked inside him. Valon didn't know what he had expected, but the gentle way Marc made love to him was not it. The backs of his eyes stung. The tingle of tears grew stronger by the second. Then their fingers linked, and their kiss turned into something beautiful. Valon lost all thought. His entire being became entwined with Marc. Marc acted like he never wanted their moment to end, and Valon didn't know what would happen when it did. The entire encounter had revealed too many things—like the real reason he always wanted Marc around and why he had opened up to Marc while incapable of doing that with anyone else. Somewhere along the line, Valon had fallen in love with Marc. He was the one person Valon felt completely free and whole with. If this ended, and Valon found out this was all Marc wanted from him, that might be the thing that pushed him over the edge. In his heart, Valon knew that would never happen. Marc had too much heart. Valon could only hope he didn't break it. What a tragedy that would be.

The growing sense of desperation inside him grew too big to ignore. Valon held his breath. His muscles tightened.

"Please, Marc."

The sound of his name must have been the final straw. Marc gave him everything. He stroked and plundered. Valon forgot the entire world existed outside of them. He whined and whimpered with need until his breath seized in his lungs. A silent scream ripped through him as his orgasm stole everything from him and replaced it with ecstasy. He barely heard the moment Marc cried his name. Valon had found his heaven. Its name was Marc.

No matter how hard he tried, Marc couldn't stop touching Valon. He had been shot to the stars. Every single thing on earth had ceased to matter. They had created a bubble, and it was like they couldn't look away from each other. If he could take a slice out of time to save forever, this was it. Few people got the chance to live their ultimate fantasy like this. He ached to hang on and for the night to never end.

"I have a bad feeling you'll pretend this didn't happen tomorrow." Marc was so shocked by the words, he didn't interrupt. "You'll worry you don't look professional. It'll embarrass you when people might think this is the typical celebrity sleeping with their bodyguard. You'll be super respectful in public and only touch me in private."

Marc found his voice. "Damn. You just summed up all the fears I have about you. I hope you'll let me touch you all the time."

A luminous smile popped to Valon's lips, showing off his dimples. "What's wrong with us?"

Marc snorted out a quick chuckle. "Probably a lot, but I don't care. You matter to me." He felt his face heat and couldn't stop it. "Actually, you're all I think about."

Valon's smile never dimmed. "You matter to me too." His expression changed. A line appeared between his eyebrows. "It just occurred to me. Could you get fired over this?"

Marc shrugged. "I have no clue. Did they fire Kash? It doesn't really matter. I'd rather be with you exactly like this than work for Steel. As much as I like the guy, no one matters as much as you."

Valon scooted closer. "I'll just hire you directly. It's not like I need their services." He kept coming until Marc rolled onto his back and Valon straddled his body.

Marc fought to keep up his end of the conversation. Valon's body felt too good pressed against him. "You kind of do. I know I stick with you even on my days off, but I'm distracted those days. It's different when I know someone else is hanging around, so I don't have to split my attention. I'm not your only guard."

Valon looked taken aback for a second before he smiled so brightly, it had to hurt. "You know what? I'm a spoiled brat. Not once have I noticed anyone else hanging around. I also never thought about your needing days off. How terrible is that? I really assumed you were mine twenty-four seven."

Marc couldn't resist touching him. He smoothed his hands down Valon's back. "You didn't assume wrong. I am yours twenty-four seven."

Valon went from smiling to serious in an instant. His expression made Marc's dick stir. “You really are.” His lips swept Marc’s lips. “I’m sorry I didn’t notice.” He lightly kissed Marc again. “But I promise I’ve noticed everything else about you.”

God, Marc hoped that wasn’t true. If Valon ever saw beneath his mask to the sickeningly addicted piece of shit he actually was, he would do everything to get away from him. Now Marc knew what it was like to own Valon’s body. Valon would never escape him now.

A gasp escaped Marc when Valon moved to lick his nipple. Every voluntary touch Valon gave him was sexy as fuck. His entire body was a live wire. He fought not to squirm as Valon kissed and licked his way down Marc’s torso. Marc was torn. While he loved the direction things seemed to be headed, there was a part of him that hated the idea of Valon lowering himself to suck Marc's dick. Was Marc fucked in the head? Yes. Before he talked himself off the edge, Marc's cock was in Valon's mouth. The sound that came from Marc sounded animalistic. It was as if he blacked out and yet still sprang into action. He had Valon completely turned where he could repay the favor with no memory of how. Marc couldn't think straight any longer. The bliss of sucking Valon's dick made the world disappear. Nothing existed but pleasuring Valon. Ten minutes ago, Marc would have sworn he was too drained to move. Now he played Valon's body, using everything in his toolbox to make Valon fly. When cum filled his mouth, Marc slipped farther into insanity. Valon should be terrified. Marc was capable of doing anything to keep him.

Chapter Seven

Truth be told, Marc expected things would be awkward for a little while as people realized they were together. Instead, no one batted an eye. Marc got the feeling everyone had assumed they had been a couple the entire time. Literally nothing changed around them. All the new experiences were reserved for them. The way Valon looked at him now and the way he always touched Marc were surreal as hell for him. It was like he was in a coma and trapped inside the most amazing dream.

He sat outside the sound booth, watching the band record their new album. The music was awesome, as always. Marc got the feeling he would soon have a few new favorites. Being proud of Valon was as familiar as breathing. Every day, his obsession grew. He wasn't sure he could handle a single night of Valon being out of his sight.

Marc's phone buzzed with an incoming text. He tried to keep one eye on the band while checking his phone.

Unknown Caller: *You son of a bitch. I know you're the reason I can't see or even talk to my son.*

Marc snorted and immediately blocked Ry. His desperation was growing. Valon had gotten three glorious months of peace, thanks to Steel and changing studios. Unfortunately, he felt the way Ry was getting close to heading in a new direction. Desperation made people do rash things. The longer Ry went without torturing Valon, the more dangerous he would become. As far as Marc had noticed, Valon hadn't realized how much time had passed without a word from his tormentor. Marc made sure Valon didn't notice anything other than him. He was a glutton for Valon. Marc made sure he knew it every second of the day. Still, this had to be addressed.

Marc was alone, so he called. A text was a trail that would follow him.

"Hey. What's up?"

Marc dove in the second he could. “Ry’s found my number. I blocked him, but it feels a lot like time is running out.”

“Don’t worry. It’s as good as taken care of.”

“That’s all I need to hear.” Marc disconnected the call just as Valon left the booth.

Valon sat on his knee. “Hey. Who was that?”

Marc’s smile was real. Reality didn’t touch him when he held Valon. “I was just checking on things at home.”

Valon perked up. “Speaking of our home. We should make that official, don’t you think? We should move your things to my room.”

God, he was everything. Marc nodded along. "I love that idea, but not tonight. Are you finished?"

"Yep. We've done as much as we can for now."

Bond strolled out last. He was all smiles as he headed their way. "Marc! It's always great to see you. How did you like the new album?"

Marc's smile matched Bond's. He actually kind of liked Bond. He reminded Marc of a lot of people he had grown up with. "I think all of you are about to be a whole lot richer."

Bond clapped his hands and rubbed them together. "Damn straight." He focused on Valon. "Keep the throat in shape. We'll meet back here next Wednesday."

Valon nodded. "Sounds good." They shook hands before Bond left them alone. Valon's sexy eyes moved back to Marc. "Back to where we left off. Why not tonight?"

Marc stood, forcing Valon to his feet. He took Valon's hand. "I have a surprise for you." With Valon's hand in his, he led Valon outside to the car. "While you were getting ready this morning, I stashed a couple of things." He popped the trunk and watched as Valon peered inside.

"What's that?"

Marc pulled out one suit. "They're inflatable costumes. See, they have air that blows through them, so we're not frying while we're dancing."

Valon didn't show any reaction. "We're going dancing?"

Even though he couldn't get a read on Valon, he didn't backpedal. Valon loved dancing at the club, and he hadn't been since Marc seemingly ruined it for him. It was time to fix that. "Yep. The last time we were at Affinity, Zeus pointed out it was only a matter of time before someone saw me watching you and put two and two together. I can't let you get mobbed, but you're allowed some freedom and fun. Let's put these on and grab that independence for you."

Valon still looked skeptical. "You still realize Affinity is like a sex club, right? I love you, but you don't strike me as wanting to be in a place like that."

Everything inside Marc was frozen with hope and fear. "Did you just say you love me?"

Valon rolled his eyes. "How did you not know that by now? Damn. I know you're not dumb."

Marc blinked. Valon really could be such a handful sometimes. He was definitely a brat. But he didn't know what to call this. "Um. I didn't know that because you've never said that. You know I'd never assume a damn thing. I know I'm just along for the ride and nowhere near good enough for you."

Valon punched him.

Marc didn't see it coming. It was a good shot too. It was just his arm, but Valon was in good shape, and he hadn't held back. Marc rubbed his arm. "Goddamn, Valon."

Valon looked enraged. "Stop saying shit like that. If you're not in love with me, you can say that. You don't have to force me to listen to some bullshit lies about you not being good enough."

Marc knew there was a way he should react, but instead, he was actually pretty turned on. He crowded Valon's space. Marc's hands moved from Valon's waist to his ass. Fuck, he was amazing and felt so good in his arms. He felt the intensity rolling off him like steam. "Oh, I'm sickeningly in love with you. I'm also fully aware that the odds of us meeting and you falling in love with me are astronomical. But you're in my arms." He hauled Valon closer so he could feel how hard he was for him. "I have you now, and I'll be damned if those odds ever take you from me." He kissed Valon. Marc felt around until he found one of the costumes. "Put this on. There's nothing I want more than to take you to a sex club, dance all night, and then take you the way I'm dying to do right now."

Valon looked dazed as hell and aroused. So fucking aroused. Marc almost abandoned his plans. Valon stared at Marc's mouth, nearly crippling him. "Okay."

An evil type of happiness rose inside him. He could and would be every fucking thing Valon needed. Even if that meant fucking Valon in some dumbass costume in front of a room full of kinky strangers, Marc was his man.

Valon had to admit; the costumes Marc chose were cooler for dancing. He wasn't sweating nearly as much. Valon had never actually seen Marc dance. It turned out, for such a huge guy, he had some moves. Valon couldn't stop smiling. It was a hell of a lot more fun to party with someone than alone. Plus, it was Marc. Anything and everything felt healthier with him. It was crazy, and he knew his happiness shouldn't rely on someone else. But Marc made him feel so freaking alive, and he woke up every day ready to see what happened next. His life had never been like this. Valon was almost ashamed considering that the people closest to him had tried saving him. Marc was the one. Every day, he woke up and rescued Valon from a life that choked him. He would probably drop dead if he lost this.

The music slowed. It was a bit awkward to hold each other in their costumes. Valon wasn't about to let any of that bullshit stop him from being in Marc's arms. That was his favorite place.

"Thank you for this."

Marc snuggled closer. "You never have to thank me. There's nowhere else I'd rather be than anywhere at all with you."

Fuck. They felt so fucking healthy. Valon couldn't stop thinking that. He didn't deserve this, but he wouldn't turn down this amazing relationship that had fallen from the sky and into his lap.

"I'm going to have to ask you to leave. I don't know who let you in, but you're on our banned list."

The loud, angry-sounding words were spoken so closely to them, at first, Valon thought they were meant for him. Luckily, he caught a quick glance when Ry looked the other way. Security was homed in on him.

"How can I be banned from someplace I've never been? That's crazy. I'm just here to find my son."

The huge guy trying to shuffle Ry toward the door looked disgusted. "Eww, dude. You have problems."

Ry growled. “Not like that. His car is out front. I...”

Valon didn’t hear the rest. Marc had subtly danced him away, putting some distance between Ry and them.

“Well, I guess we’d better find another way home.”

Zeus appeared beside them, dancing with his husband. He was too smooth. No one who looked at them would think they conversed. “When Judas has Ry off the dance floor and distracted at the front door, we’ll slowly dance our way to the back door. We’ll exchange keys. Take my car, and I’ll bring yours home tomorrow.”

Thankfully, Marc spoke on their behalf while Valon shut down. He didn’t even hear what was said. A chill had sunk into his bones. It pissed Valon off, but the shaking set in. He ground his back teeth. Things had been so peaceful. They'd been good. He hated the fact that Ry still made him react this way. Valon always swung wildly between furious, annoyed, and scared as hell when it came to Ry. Plus, he was just sad. Ry was supposed to love him. Valon had spent the first half of his life trying to be perfect so maybe Ry would want him around. He supposed there would always be a part of him that craved the love he just couldn't get.

Valon let himself get manhandled and shuffled around. Marc became the body-guard again. He kept Valon safe purely by using his size. Marc's head stuck out of the costume, and he never stopped checking their surroundings. Valon was inside a car he didn't recognize in no time. The windows were darkly tinted.

He didn't think Ry would see him even if he stood inches outside the door.

Marc climbed behind the wheel. Valon couldn't look at anything else. He felt like he should have thanked Zeus. There were probably a dozen things he should have done or said. Instead, he turned mute and stared at the man he loved. Marc looked like a different person. He looked like someone Valon wouldn't want to meet in a dark alley. Logically, Valon understood Marc's intensity was all for him. He was in work mode. But this wasn't the first time he had caught glimpses of the person next to him, and he kind of scared Valon. Sometimes, he worried that coldness could turn his way. Marc looked capable of murdering someone. His size had only ever frightened Valon once—the last time they had been here. Unfortunately, Valon saw how quickly Marc could transform into a weapon. He didn't know if he felt safer or in more danger.

Halfway home, Marc stopped constantly checking the mirrors. "I don't think we were followed, but Ry still knows where you live. He'll probably waste time waiting for you to come out. I have a feeling he'll head straight to the house when he gets tired of staring at your car. We need to get inside before that happens." Marc glanced his way, as if checking to see if Valon listened. A laugh burst from him, making him look like Valon's Marc again. Marc visibly tried to get himself under control. "I'm sorry." He wiped his eyes. "I just looked over, and a unicorn looked back at me, and I don't know." His hand lifted from the steering wheel before dropping again. “It just struck me as hilarious.” He sighed. “Damn. I needed that.”

Valon’s shoulders relaxed. He knew Marc. “I’m here to serve.”

Marc took his hand and held it. “You’re so fucking strong. You know that, right? Most people would’ve freaked out, but you stayed calm and did everything right. You should be really proud of yourself. Nothing can break you.”

As much as Marc’s words warmed his chest, they weren’t true. Not at all. He felt precariously close to breaking down. He fought against all his old coping methods. The shaking got harder as the shock wore off.

Marc glanced his way. Concern etched his features. “Oh fuck. Are you okay? I can't check your emotions with that costume blocking your face. We're almost home. I've got you."

His panic attack took him out. He barely noticed pulling into the garage or when Marc scooped him from the car and carried him inside. In a detached way, he heard Marc quickly giving everyone a heads up to be on the lookout tonight. Then he was up the stairs, and Valon found himself underneath a deluge of hot water. His mind slowly cleared as Marc rubbed his arms, obviously trying to warm him.

"It's okay. I swear. No one is getting near you. I have you. If anyone wants to hurt you, they'll have to kill me."

Marc finally came into full focus. Valon couldn't look away from the Hawaiian-blue eyes that had captivated him from the first time they met. “You’d never hurt me, right?”

Marc looked as if all the fight left him. “No, baby. I’d rather step into traffic than hurt you.”

The vise crushing his chest loosened. This was Marc. He knew Marc. Marc loved him like no one else had before. All this darkness was because he loved Valon and took keeping him safe seriously. He knew that. Valon shook his head. “I’m sorry. I don’t know why I asked that. You love me. I feel it.” Honestly, he felt a little dumb now that the shock had worn completely off. He swiped his hand over his eyes. “Jesus. I really don’t know what happened. Everything has just been going so well, and Ry always takes everything from me. I’m just—”

Marc shuffled closer and kissed him, cutting off the new downward spiral. Everything vanished except the man who held him. Then the slow realization came. They were both nude. Marc was right there. Valon's body knew what it was like to have Marc's body.

"I need you." Valon whispered the plea between kisses. As always, Marc never let him down.

The second the words left his mouth, he was swept into Marc's arms again. A trail of water followed them. Valon's skin chilled, but not his desire. Still soaking wet and with no concern for the bed they slept in, Marc had him squished in the pile of cozy blankets. He barely felt Marc move away. Marc was back in seconds with lubed fingers. He toyed with Valon's asshole while kissing and biting his skin. Valon fought for air like a man who had almost drowned. That was exactly what happened when Marc had pulled him off the ledge. Then Marc was inside him. Every problem and worry he ever faced vanished. His whole being focused on the dick in his ass. It was rare for Marc to treat him like anything other than glass. He always made love to Valon like he was precious and fragile. When Valon was in charge, he always took Marc's cock fast and hard. He loved every way they came together. Tonight was different. Marc fucked him. There was no other description. Valon had begged for Marc to take the darkness from him. He loved the way Marc obeyed.

All Valon could do was cling to Marc any way he could while Marc pounded him.

Gasps, moans, and whimpers were the only sounds he could make. He wanted to tell Marc how much he loved him. Valon needed to say how much Marc had changed his life for the better. Marc deserved all the words of love, appreciation, and praise. Valon had nothing but guttural noises to give. He needed exactly this.

Valon's fingers dug into Marc's skin. His entire lower half wound tighter and tighter. Valon's muscles were completely seized. He held his breath and gritted his teeth. Valon knew the greatest orgasm was on the edge of the horizon. Marc roared as he came. It was sexy as fuck and apparently what his body waited for. Valon blew. A spasm from his soul made his entire body jump. He fought to stay alive while the pleasure rocked through him.

His dick jerked, shooting his cum. Valon squirmed, trying to get every millisecond of ecstasy. He didn't even know what Marc did while he was stuck in heaven.

The sensation of his neck being kissed cut through the brain fog. Valon's hands became more aware of the body he held.

"I love you." The confession came from his soul, and even he heard the power of his claim.

Marc still kissed him, making his way to Valon's mouth when he responded. "I love you too. You make me want everything with you." He covered Valon's mouth before he could respond, but yeah. Valon wanted everything with him too.

Chapter Eight

Warm lips brushed his nape. Still half asleep, Valon was already smiling. He peeked one eye open and glanced at the time. Nine a.m. Damn. That was early when he had nowhere to be. He couldn't complain, though. The sexiest lips he had ever encountered currently trailed down his neck. Valon had kissed a lot of men. Women too, to be honest. Marc was hands down the sexiest mouth he had ever enjoyed. He kissed Valon like it was his only job, and he loved it more than oxygen. His passion was all-consuming. Within five seconds of Marc's mouth on his body, Valon would do anything Marc wanted.

Marc's hand smoothed over Valon's hip. There was no missing Marc's erection between them.

A shaky breath escaped him. Valon leaned into the body against his back. It was empowering as hell to know he was the reason Marc acted as if he couldn't get enough.

Marc's hand moved to stroke Valon's cock. His hips rolled, humping Valon's ass. He didn't speak. Neither did Valon. Heavy breathing was the only sound that filled the room.

Valon reached over his head and grabbed Marc's hair. He couldn't risk Marc getting away. It didn't take long for him to seek more from Marc's palm. Desperation was quick to take over. When it came to Marc, his arousal was way more than sexual. Marc was in his heart and had set up shop inside his soul. Every encounter felt deeply personal on a level he had never experienced before. It was like every time they had any sort of sexual encounter, the act was more than for the pleasure. They were getting closer, building something.

Marc's movements quickened. All thoughts disappeared. He was deeply in love and didn't plan to look back. They had a future. Valon wanted it. Pressure built. He couldn't stop whimpering. He didn't care how he looked or sounded. Valon was desperate for the release Marc offered. When his orgasm hit, Valon couldn't make a sound. His body twitched with pleasure.

Marc's body moved faster against him. Valon swore he would feel Marc's release as his own. That was how connected he felt. When Marc cried out against his shoulder, Valon's eyes closed. He savored every sensation. It took Valon a second to realize he was crying. Everything had been such shit for so long that Marc felt like this beautiful miracle that breathed new life into his weary soul. He didn't feel worthy. That wasn't something he could explain. He had just spent so much time being selfish or not sticking up for himself. He had been small where it counted the most. Everything the world saw and loved was a fake version of Valon. Marc loved the real him, and the relief was almost painful.

“Shhh. Don’t cry. I’ve got you.”

Valon's breath shook when he tried to sniffle. He felt a little dumb. Valon hadn’t realized how obvious his tears were. He tried to explain, but no sound emerged.

Marc held him tighter. “Your body is just letting go of a lot of long-carried tension. But I’ve got you. You don’t need to pretend when you’re with me. I don’t expect you to be the rock star. You don’t have to twist into knots to deal with the bad things. I’m here, and I love you so fucking much. The real, beautiful you.”

Valon found his voice, even though it shook. “I know. That’s why I’m crying. I never thought I’d find you.”

The way Marc squeezed Valon against his chest slowly leached the poison that had been killing him. Every minute that passed in Marc's hold was a minute closer to a flawless life.

A watery laugh escaped Valon. "Okay. I'm ready to face the day now."

Marc chuckled against his shoulder. "You've already conquered me. Next step, the world."

Valon smiled. "I've already done that. You're my world."

For a moment, total silence followed his words. It was like Valon had stolen Marc's ability to talk or breathe. He sniffed. The sound melted Valon's heart. Marc cleared his throat. "You make me believe I could have things I never thought I would. I gave up on a lot a long time ago. You have no idea how much you feel like a miracle to me."

Valon had no idea why Marc felt that way, but he was happy that it seemed like they were saving each other. "I think I want to work on a new song today."

Marc kissed his neck. "We should get ready, then. Let's leave this mess we've made for the cleaning crew and get downstairs to your studio."

Valon chuckled as he rolled and stole a quick kiss. "I love this plan." While they used one of the record label's studios for recording, Valon had his own for creating and perfecting new music. Marc made him want to create again. For that alone, he could marry the guy.

There was no describing the way Marc loved watching Valon live his dream. The stars in Marc's eyes never disappeared. He could spend the rest of his life watching Valon thrive. Just knowing he was part of the magic was like waking up every day to the best dream. He couldn't see what Valon wrote, but he still watched. Valon would scratch in his notebook and then strum a few chords while humming. Every few seconds, he stopped and scribbled some more. The entire process was sexy as fuck to watch unfold. A silver curl kept falling across Valon's eye. He kept swatting it away or tucking the strand behind his ear. Marc was fascinated by that curl. He swore he felt the soft lock between his fingers. Marc knew how that hair smelled. He would have thought getting to know Valon would dim his terrifying obsession. The opposite was true. Marc had progressed to a point where he scared himself. One way or another, Valon would always be his. Marc felt the intense insanity roiling inside him. There was no slowing the way he felt. Each day, he sank deeper. Valon was his forever, one way or the other. He could never let Valon touch anyone else. Marc had done too much. Came too far. He would have to be put down like an animal if Valon tried to walk away.

Valon's chin lifted.

Marc scrambled to hide his crazed expression. He became the teddy bear Valon thought he needed. A sweet smile passed over Valon's lips, and he went back to writing. Valon didn't realize what he truly needed was a grizzly. Someone who would kill for him without mercy. Someone who protected his peace with any force necessary. Marc was that bear. Admittedly, he hadn't expected to enjoy being soft for Valon quite so much. It turned out all the ways he played at being a lovable protector were actually part of his personality. He hadn't known that because there was only one Valon. It seemed he could be gentle when he wanted to be. He kind of loved being that guy for Valon. Marc swallowed a bark of laughter as the truth hit. Valon had trained him like a wild animal. He gave Marc all the rewards and treats for loving him the way he wanted. That was fine. As long as he still got that reward, Marc could be anyone. It wouldn't be the first time he had transformed his whole existence into someone new. This was worth it.

Valon leaned toward the mic. "Why do you look so much like the cat that ate the canary?"

An out-of-control grin stretched Marc's lips. "Maybe I'm plotting ways to eat that canary."

A loud bark of laughter rang from the sound booth walls. Everything inside Marc hummed. Happiness looked irresistible on Valon.

Nathaniel appeared in the doorway. “Your father and Mr. Kash are waiting to see you in the front sitting room.”

Valon looked puzzled. “That’s odd. They never come here, especially without calling first.”

Marc stood. “Maybe they were in the neighborhood.”

Valon moved to his feet and set his guitar aside. “Why would they be hanging out in L.A.?”

“Why does anyone?” Marc infused as much humor as possible.

Valon tossed him a laughing look as he headed for the door. Marc hung back and followed on his heels. His gaze ate up every inch of Valon. Fuck. He looked amazing in jeans that looked like they were aged to perfection. More likely, they were just expensive. It didn't matter which. Those jeans cupped the sexiest fucking ass on the planet. Marc wanted to dig his fingertips into those cheeks while he helped Valon ride him at the perfect pace. Thoughts of all the things he could do to Valon's body carried him all the way to the sitting room.

Ledger sat looking a lot more serious than normal. Kash stood next to his seat, looking like the killer he was. Yeah. Marc knew everything about him. No one got anywhere near Valon without Marc knowing every detail of their lives.

"Hey, Dad. I didn't know you were coming over today. I would've planned dinner or something."

A sad-looking smile tugged at Ledger's lips. The air grew heavy. "You should probably sit down."

"Oh no. That doesn't sound good." Valon moved to sit on the loveseat across from Ledger's wingback chair. Marc intended to fill the spot beside him.

Kash gently took his arm and steered him toward the door. "We should leave them to talk."

Valon tossed him a scared look.

"Just yell if you need me."

Valon nodded.

Marc lost sight of him as Kash shuffled him inside the kitchen. Kash headed straight for the fridge while Nathaniel looked scandalized. Guests simply didn't open the refrigerator on his well-oiled ship.

“What’s up, Nate?”

Nathaniel didn’t respond. He left the room.

Kash grabbed two beers from the fridge. He laughed as he passed one Marc’s way. “Well, that had the desired effect. We’re alone.”

Marc twisted the cap off the bottle and tossed it onto the island. “What’s up?” He took a swig as he waited for whatever Kash planned to hit him with.

“Ry’s dead.”

Marc shrugged. “Good riddance.” He took another drink. He had a bad feeling about where this was headed. Kash didn’t look as friendly as he always did.

“You don’t seem surprised.”

Marc leaned back against the counter behind him. “I’m surprised. I just don’t care. He was a piece of shit. The world is better off without him.”

Kash continued eyeing him in a way that made the hair stand on the back of Marc’s neck. “I know who you are, by the way.”

Marc pulled a confused face. He was an excellent actor. “Yeah. No shit. You hired me to be Valon’s guard. We’ve had a while now to get to know each other. I fucking hope you know who I am.”

Kash’s stare turned more intense, as if seeking weaknesses in Marc's words. “Yeah. I did that. But then something about you ate at my gut. It’s your eyes. At first, I thought you just had that everyday nice-guy look. But the more often I saw you, the more those eyes scratched the back of my brain. They're your dad's eyes."

Marc pulled even more confusion into his vibe. "Yeah. I don't look anything like my dad."

"Maybe not, except for those eyes."

Marc didn't show an ounce of concern even though he knew he was cornered. "So? Who is this mysterious dad?" There was still a chance Kash was wrong. He wouldn't out himself willingly.

"John Slaughter Campbell."

A loud snort burst from him that nearly had beer spewing out his nose. Kash had chosen a hell of a time to say that. Now his sinuses burned. "There're people who still call him that? I thought the press had chosen something different." Marc shook his head, still trying to keep from laughing. He pulled out a stool and sat. "What's the point of this conversation?"

Kash shrugged and grabbed a stool across from him. "I've known for a while, but Valon has become a whole new person thanks to you. While I have no idea what you did, the change has made Ledger sleep better. When Ledger sleeps better, I sleep better. You feel me? I don't think you mean him harm. But I also don't know what your game is, and I don't like that."

"There's no game." He had already won. "Why does there have to be a game? He's happy. That makes me happy. Life keeps running smoothly."

Kash set his beer aside and sighed. "For Ledger's sake, I want to believe you don't mean any harm. Unfortunately, I know all about you, and it's bloody. It's always been in your genes to cause harm." Kash's gaze sharpened. "But it's always been my job to be just as dangerous. If I see any signs you intend to hurt him or exploit him in any way, I'd really hate to pit my insanity against yours. But I have no mercy when it comes to Ledger. I'd bet on me."

Marc couldn't stop his eye roll. "I don't think you realize how dramatic you sound. Did you forget to look into my life at all, or did you stop with my dad? I ended up in a decent foster home, got good grades, went to college on a football scholarship, and landed a career I love. It seems kind of unfair to judge me for the sins of my father."

Kash snorted. "So that family who took you in both worked directly below a CEO who stole a lot of money from them. He turned up dead not long after you were taken in. That high school where you got such good grades had two teachers go missing a month after you graduated. The town where you went to college had a few mysterious deaths while you were there. While I can't say those had anything to do with you, it's an odd coincidence for you to always be there."

Marc couldn't stop smiling. He shook his head. "I'm pretty sure those two teachers ran off together. They were both married to other people and still narrowly missed getting caught in compromising positions nearly every day. Just because my dad is a murderer doesn't mean I am."

Kash cocked his head to one side, openly studying him. "No, but you have it in you. You could do it. It took me a while to recognize what I saw in you that made me so certain you could save Valon, but I see it now. It's me. I see myself when I look at you. That crazed obsession. The way you can mimic feelings and personalities, becoming whoever it takes to get whatever job done with zero remorse."

Marc chuckled. "Ouch. I have feelings."

"Do any of them extend to anyone beyond Valon? I need to know he's not in danger with you. Right now, I'm not so sure. I mean, Ry—"

Marc felt everything inside him harden. He became the person Kash feared he might be. "Ry was a vile piece of shit who literally tortured his own son every time you and Ledger weren't looking. Neither of you bothered to notice while you were wrapped up in each other. The moment Valon got a single thing Ry could take that he hadn't already, he spent his free time tormenting Valon the only way he still could: blackmail."

"Whoa. What?"

Marc couldn't stop. It was too late. Kash had unlocked a rage Marc had worked hard to tamp down. "It came to me to be the savior Valon needed. Everyone else has been too busy overlooking him as a dramatic, spoiled rock star with no real problems. He should fucking hate you all for the way you left him in pain and then to drown. How very fucking dare you come to me, accusing me of being the danger. Looks to me, all the people who should've loved him and saved him are the real danger. Don't worry. I've got him." Marc heard the rage and barely contained ugliness that ran in his blood. He couldn't stop it. He had been set free of his self-imposed restraints. Kash didn't want this fight.

Kash looked genuinely hurt. "He hurt Valon and blackmailed him? Why didn't he say something? I never would've stood aside and let that happen."

"Yet you did." Marc didn't care if he dug into the wound he had just created. "But as I said, there's no need to think about any of this ever again. I want the job you failed. He's in good hands."

Kash looked devastated.

The hair on the back of Marc's neck tingled. The air in the room changed. Valon came into view, looking shell-shocked.

He headed straight into Marc's arms. Marc became the guy Valon needed. "I heard, baby. Are you okay?"

He felt Valon shrug. His voice muffled against Marc's chest as he spoke. "I don't know how I feel right now. Tell me how to feel? I don't even know anymore. It's too... I just..." Valon shrugged again. Ledger spoke to Kash in a quiet tone. Valon whispered, keeping his words for Marc's ears. "I'm relieved as hell, and I don't know where to go with that."

Marc held him tighter and kissed the top of his head. "We'll figure it out. I'm here." His gaze met Kash's over the top of Valon's head as he made the claim. "I've always got you."

Valon released a relieved-sounding breath against his chest. "Thank God."

Marc didn't revert to his old self. He wanted to be who Valon needed now. Marc understood there were mixed feelings. Even though this was for the best, Ry had been someone Valon had spent years desperately hoping would love him. There was always a strange line between love and hate when dealing with someone who should've meant something. When the shock passed, Ry's death would be a huge weight lifted from Valon. Marc was here to love him through all the good and bad times. He would make sure Valon only had good times from here on out. Valon would see. Marc would make his life perfect. He had all the tools to do it, and he wasn't scared to use them.

Chapter Nine

Somewhere between asleep and awake, Valon savored the sensation of Marc gently running his fingers through his hair. From the pillow on Marc's lap, Valon accepted the peace he offered. He kept his breathing even. Valon had slept more since Marc began sleeping with him at night than he ever had before. It was probably wrong how much he adored the way Marc spoiled him. Valon needed to sit down and come up with a plan to make Marc feel as special as he made Valon feel. Today, he didn't want to think about anything. Ry's death was at the back of his mind, waiting to pounce. Every thought he had made him feel like a bad person and torn. There was a lot of guilt associated with how he felt about Ry being gone. Maybe his feelings were justified. But sometimes, Valon wondered if he was a cold person. It was a little scary how quickly he could slam the door on his heart. He was damn good at walking away and never looking back. Life had handed him the chance to finally do that with Ry. That was exactly what Valon planned to do.

"How is he?"

At the quiet question, Valon peeked his eyes open for half a second. Just long enough to know who spoke.

Marc kept stroking his hair. “He’s okay. Tell me what happened.”

A moment passed. He didn’t know if German checked to see if he was asleep or simply shrugged.

“He was jogging and ran right into traffic. I guess he didn’t check to see if it was safe to cross. A woman on her way to work couldn’t stop quickly enough to avoid him. She’s pretty shaken up. They don’t intend to charge her with anything, since Ry wasn’t at a crosswalk. She wasn’t at fault. They took her to the hospital, though. It seems she’s a huge mess over this.”

“I imagine so. That’s a lot to live with.”

Valon was confused. Why didn’t Marc know how Ry died? He had been in the kitchen with Kash for a while before Valon sought him out. Why was German the one getting that information for Marc? He had been glued to Valon's side the entire day. When did he have time to ask German to find out for him? He could have just asked Valon. Maybe he hadn't wanted to put that burden on Valon. Still, it just seemed odd.

"Since you don't need me any longer, Steel plans to reassign me."

Why would they suddenly not need German any longer?

"If you want to stay on here, I'm sure Valon would be fine with that."

Valon heard the smile in German's voice when he responded. "I appreciate that, but you know me. I don't stay anywhere too long. Hopping from state to state keeps life interesting. I didn't mind so much when it came to guarding Jathan. His busy game schedule kept us moving. I'm not built to stay in one place for too long."

"Okay. I get it." Marc sounded resigned if not a little unhappy. Valon had known the pair were friends, so he kind of got it. But Steel was right; they already had plenty of security on property. German wasn't really needed here. He hadn't understood why he had been sent in the first place. Not that it mattered. He didn't run that shit.

"I should probably start packing. When Valon wakes up, be sure to let him know it was an honor."

"I will."

Silence followed. He drifted closer to sleep.

"How long do you plan to pretend you're sleeping?"

Valon never opened his eyes. "I'm not pretending." Even he heard how slurred his words were.

"Good. I love you. You need to rest."

"Love you too." His voice sounded far away, as if someone else spoke in the room. He kept drifting a few seconds at a time. Valon had no idea why he couldn't commit to the nap. His mind got the best of him. "Who do you think will plan his funeral?"

"I don't know. Does he have any living relatives?"

Valon really had to dig deep. He had dissociated for most of his childhood. A vague memory rose. "He has a sister in the Midwest somewhere. I don't really know her. She never came around."

"There you go." Marc's hand moved from Valon's hair to his back. He rubbed slow circles between Valon's shoulder blades.

"Mhmm. That feels good. Do you think I should offer to pay for it? I have the money, and I don't want anyone else to have to shoulder that burden. His sister didn't come around for a reason, I'm sure."

"If no one claims his body, the state will bury him." Marc sounded like there was nothing he cared less about than Ry's death. That was fair. Valon should feel the same. He was so confused.

Valon was awake now. He felt defeated. It seemed even Marc didn't understand his mixed feelings. There was a sliver of him that hurt over this situation.

The ridiculous child inside him, who had dreamed Ry might love him someday, wanted to cry about Ry's passing. But Valon couldn't, and he felt like he was expected to feel nothing. For the most part, he did. But feeling like he had no one to talk to about the small child inside him was isolating. Valon tried harder to shut down his mind.

"If you want to plan the funeral, I'll do it with you. Whatever you need right now, I'm here. I know you're dealing with a lot of mixed-up emotions. No matter how much of a monster he was, ultimately, he was your dad. He's gone. There's nothing more he can do to harm you now. But if you need to do something to help close the book on him, I'll be by your side every step."

Goddamn it. Marc always said the right things. It was like he could read Valon's mind. "I think I need to handle it."

Marc ran his fingers through Valon's hair again. "Okay. I'm with you."

Wow, he really was and Valon could breathe again. One way or another, Valon had to keep Marc. His life was better because Marc existed. He was safe.

Warm water poured over his hands as Marc rinsed the plate he had just washed. There was a good chance Ledger had a cleaning crew. At the very least, he probably used the dishwasher. Marc enjoyed the mundane task. He felt useful in a situation that made him feel helpless.

Ry's funeral had been... odd, to say the least. Marc couldn't think of a better way to describe everything that had gone down. First, it turned out Ry had a will and had requested to be cremated. He had also left his gym to Ledger, which made Marc wonder if all the blackmail and stalking had really been about keeping some part of Ledger. Maybe Ry had always believed Ledger would be his again in the end. It was hard to feel like there had been a funeral service at all when there was nothing more than an urn with a picture beside it. It had been a generously young picture of him. That made it even harder to connect the situation to an actual death. Even if anything had felt real, the day was way more than Ry deserved. In the smallest of ways, Marc understood how Ry had ended up resenting Valon. To his core, Ry had been a narcissistic, cheating bastard. Nothing had mattered to him more than his ego. His desire to avoid child support had left him tied down. Ry had been more than willing to gnaw off Valon's leg to be free, only to wish he had the life he destroyed back. The saddest part was, Marc imagined Ry had decided to have a child to stroke the same ego that led to his destruction. He just hadn't possessed the foresight to see how much freedom he would lose. In some ways, Marc imagined his father had done the same. Except Marc's dad had actually wanted the trophy that was Marc. Marc still didn't know which fate was worse.

"You know you don't have to wash dishes. Valon pays someone to clean." Ledger chuckled. "That keeps me torn between aggravated and frugal. He's paying for the service. It would be rude not to use it. On the other hand, it seems pretty pretentious."

Marc turned a smile Ledger's way. "As crazy as it may sound, I actually like doing dishes, especially at times like this. I don't like standing by helpless to help. So at least it's something."

Ledger nodded and leaned back against the counter where Marc worked. He crossed his arms, looking thoughtful. "You know, when I first realized Valon and you were dating, I had some huge reservations. That's nothing against you," Ledger tacked on as if not wanting to insult Marc. "In fact, it's kind of the opposite. He's blossomed so much with you being his guard and friend. Once that relationship changed, I was scared as hell of what would happen to him if you two didn't work out. We couldn't reach him before you. How bad would he be without you? But the more time that passes and the more I see you two together, I'm not as scared of that outcome. You love him. In general, you're just really good for him. I can't tell you how thankful I am for you to have brought my real son back." Ledger looked around. His expression darkened. "I fucking loathe the fact that he feels like he needs to do this. This entire day has been way more than Ry ever deserved."

Marc nodded along, finishing his last dish. "Agreed, but I'm all for whatever it takes for him to leave Ry behind. I hate the moments when I watch the happiness drain from him. Every time, I know exactly what he's thinking about. I want that to stop. He's started counseling again. I told him I would go with him. Healing has to start somewhere. I'm glad he finally confided in you. You two love each other. I don't want Valon to lose that connection."

Ledger eyed him for a moment. "Well, damn. Maybe you're the one I need to worry about. I have a feeling losing my son would wreck you."

Before he could stop it from happening, since it really wasn't the time, Marc chuckled. "I won't be losing him." Valon had exactly the same chance as an ice cube in hell of getting rid of him now.

Valon appeared behind him. His arms encircled Marc, and he kissed Marc's nape. "Why am I not surprised to find you doing something completely unnecessary? You're incapable of doing nothing."

Ledger flashed him a smile and winked. He kissed Valon's forehead. "Proud of you, kid." He walked away, leaving them alone.

Marc turned and squeezed Valon as much as he could without hurting him. "I'm proud of you too. You did something today most people would never do. You're a good person." A hell of a lot better than he was. Marc might have donated his body to one of those body farms.

"Not really. I had a thought."

"Whatever it is, I love it already." Seeing Valon smile was worth any ridiculous statement.

Valon huffed. "You don't know. Maybe you'll hate it."

That would never happen. "Go on."

"My next tour starts in two weeks. Once we're on the road, we won't get a ton of alone time. How do you feel about taking the next week and a half or so and going somewhere? It can be super touristy or completely secluded. You can choose. I've been damn near everywhere."

Like Marc would say no. "Since you've been everywhere, give me your top three favorites to choose from. I'm not well-traveled enough to pick a town from thin air."

Valon looked thoughtful for a moment. Then he brightened. They were going wherever he said first. The place obviously made him happy. "Salem is a lot of fun. It's beautiful and full of history. Ibiza is super cool. Or we could just do Disney World. I love that place."

Okay, so the choice didn't turn out to be as easy as he thought. "Well, I have no idea where Ibiza is, and I was ready to answer Salem until you got to the end. Now, I'm torn. I've never been to either place, but I know I secretly coveted Disney as a kid."

Valon shrugged. "Let's do both. We can check out Salem for a couple of days and then spend the rest of our vacation in the parks. You'll love it there. You truly are in a bubble. This is great. I'm so excited." He went up on his toes and kissed Marc. Marc practically felt the joy rolling off Valon in waves. He really hoped this wasn't some odd coping mechanism. He was past ready for Valon to always feel this way. The quicker they got started, the better.

Chapter Ten

Despite his exhaustion and horrible sunburn, Marc hadn't stopped floating on a cloud since the very first time Valon touched him. The pride in his chest grew bigger every time he watched Valon sing and dance. He was so high-energy and sexy. So fucking sexy. Words couldn't express how humbling and amazing it was to know Valon loved him. Men and women all over the country had thrown themselves at Valon for the past six months. Valon always only looked for Marc in every crowd.

The final song was always the love song Valon had written and recorded shortly before the tour started. As always, mid-song, Valon's head turned to where Marc stood in the shadows, side stage. Each and every time, Marc's hand went to his stomach, fighting back the butterflies. He had lived an odd life. Being with Valon wiped away every memory he refused to remember. He wanted this life for the rest of his days.

"You've changed him."

Marc's heart tried jumping into his throat. He had been so lost in watching Valon, Bond's loudly spoken words caught him off guard. Marc hid his reaction.

"Is that a good or a bad thing?"

Bond's smile didn't budge. It never did. "It's good. I've never seen him like this. Not even when he first hit it big. He's always dealt with black moods. I haven't seen that side of him since you appeared. It's nice."

Marc's gaze slid back toward Valon. "Good. I intend to keep him this way." His claim got lost in Valon jogging his way.

Valon kissed him. "I have to do an encore, or they'll tear this place down."

Marc didn't even wipe away the sweat Valon transferred to him with that kiss. Totally worth it. "Get back out there, then."

Valon winked and ran back on stage to cheers so loud, Marc swore the walls shook. He loved this for Valon, but he was also glad this final concert was back in L.A. Marc was ready to sleep in their bed again. With the song nearing its end, Marc turned and motioned for Ledger and Kash to follow Bond to the green room. He had spent the entire concert ignoring Kash, using his duties as an excuse to avoid him. Marc hated that Kash's words had gotten so far under his skin the last time they spoke. He had managed to avoid Kash all through Ry's memorial. It was a hell of a lot easier tonight. He loathed knowing he had lost his temper and said things he couldn't take back. That was one of the biggest reasons he kept his anger in check. Marc scared himself once everything turned red. He had always liked Kash. It sucked that things had come to this.

As always, Marc went into work mode as Valon ran off stage for the last time. Marc crowded his space and kept a close watch on every corner and face. A few people had won backstage passes from some soda company sweepstakes. They bounced in place with barely suppressed excitement. While the fans were just that, Marc knew from personal experience how far a fan would go. He was proof of that, but Marc only wanted the best things for Valon. No one else could be trusted. Valon signed shit and took selfies. He answered tons of questions and even called to wish someone's mom a happy birthday. Valon was amazing. That was why insanity flocked to him. It took forever, but the green room finally cleared, leaving only family, the band, security, and Bond to rest a minute.

Valon sat next to Ledger and chatted. Various band members broke out the alcohol. Their guards exchanged glances. It would be a long night. As always, Marc became the wallflower, watching from the sidelines. While Marc liked most people and could talk to just about anyone, this wasn't one of those situations. He was working. Valon wouldn't be safe until they were home. Marc couldn't risk relaxing.

"I think I owe you an apology."

Kash's silent appearance and words surprised Marc. The shock sounded in his tone. "Why?"

Kash smiled like he found Marc humorous. "Well, as I recall, I practically accused you of being a serial killer."

Marc kept switching between watching the door and keeping an eye on Valon. "Maybe I am."

"Damn." Kash dragged out the curse. "You really are pissed."

Marc shot him an annoyed look. "Maybe I should just assume you're a raging alcoholic since your mom was."

Kash shook his head. "I'm guessing you know everything about everyone in Valon's life. It also seems like I really do owe that apology. Things were a bit raw that night. Despite Ry being the worst person alive, Ledger was still married to the guy for twenty years, and he was still Valon's dad. The situation was a little higher stress than I even realized at the time. When things cooled, I immediately recognized I shouldn't have said any of that shit. I imagine life hasn't been easy for you. If I were in your shoes, I would've changed my name to something completely unrecognizable and moved to another country. Yet you've stood pretty damn strong."

Marc's shoulders relaxed. Now he felt guilty for holding on to this for so long. "To be fair, I might've felt the same way if the shoe was on the other foot. I know you're trying to protect your family. So am I."

Before Kash responded, Valon appeared and tucked himself beneath Marc's arm. He focused on Kash. "We'll be over the day after tomorrow for lunch. I'm so glad you guys came. We're beyond ready to get home to our bed. I'm exhausted."

Kash nodded along. He didn't look at Marc again. "Sounds great. You were amazing tonight. Seriously. Happiness looks good on you, and it showed in your performance. I'm proud of you."

Valon beamed. He truthfully looked like joy radiated from him. It was nice.

Ledger kissed Valon's temple. "Be careful going home." Ledger flashed a smile Marc's way. "It's good to see you. I appreciate you taking such good care of Valon."

"No one ever has to thank me for that."

Goodbyes were exchanged along with more promises to keep their lunch date. By the time they were in the back of the SUV, heading home, Marc's shoulders hurt from spending the whole night so tense. Not to mention all the months before that. Valon had taken on an extra travel guard for the tour, but Marc hadn't realized how vulnerable Valon was until he joined a tour.

He felt Valon shake. Marc's gaze dropped to Valon's hands. They visibly shook before Valon clasped them so hard, his knuckles turned white. Marc went on full alert.

"Are you okay?" He covered Valon's hands with his. "Tell me what you need."

Valon chuckled as he met Marc's gaze. His teeth chattered, making Marc lose his breath. He couldn't handle anything being wrong. "I didn't grab my jacket off the bus. It's fucking freezing."

Marc didn't waste time diving for the rear climate control system. He turned the heat on full blast and took off his shirt.

“Here, use this as a blanket until you warm up.”

Valon’s eyes swam with laughter. “Thank you. It’s not that big of a deal.”

“It is to me.”

At his serious tone, Valon’s smile slipped away. “This really bothers you, doesn’t it?”

Marc tried not to squirm in discomfort. “Of course. You’re my everything.”

Valon’s gaze moved over Marc’s face, as if working out a puzzle in his head. “You should marry me.”

Everything inside Marc went still. He didn’t even breathe. Valon couldn’t play with him like that. Marc wasn’t that sane. Marc tried to respond, but no sound emerged. He cleared his throat and tried again. “Is that something you’d want?” He couldn’t let himself hope.

Valon clasped his hands again. This time, the gesture looked like a nervous one. It was Valon’s turn to clear his throat. “Is it something you’d consider?”

Was he fucking crazy? “Hell yeah.”

A smile exploded across Valon’s face. “Good, because I’m asking.”

The shock was thick, but so was the excitement. “I could keep saying ‘hell yeah’ all night, if you’d like. That answer’s not changing.”

For a moment, they simply stared at each other, as if basking in the reality of their conversation.

Valon ended up being the one to break the silence. “I really fucking love you.”

Marc realized something he had refused to let himself believe. Valon did love him. That adoration was in every word and touch. Deed and song. He didn't have a good track record of things working out for him. But this was real, and he couldn't contain it. Marc attacked. He had Valon in his arms, taking the kiss he wanted. Marc didn't give a shit about their driver. This was their moment.

Still, Marc's anxiety got the best of him. He spoke between kisses, needing Valon to know he wouldn't go anywhere no matter what. "If you're just caught up in the moment or whatever, you can backtrack. I won't be angry. Hurt maybe," he added because he couldn't completely lie.

Valon settled down. He clung to Marc's side. "I'm not caught up in the moment.

There should be a ring waiting for you when we get home. I contacted a famous jewelry maker for a custom piece a few weeks back. I hadn't decided how I would ask, since I wanted to do something romantic. Sorry you got screwed out of that. I'm not a patient person."

Oh, Marc was aware, and he kind of loved that about him. "No. This was perfect." It truly was. Valon's proposal proved how much he wanted this. His inability to wait was the best way to ask as far as Marc was concerned. Marc didn't know if this would really happen. If so, he didn't know how long Valon would want to wait. He imagined it took time to draw up a prenup and whatnot. Marc would sign anything. He was getting the only thing he wanted from Valon: Valon.

Between his concert and engagement, Valon rode on cloud nine. He couldn't put into words the way Marc had changed his life. Changed him. Unfortunately, Valon wasn't always as sure Marc could say the same. Several times during the tour, he had watched Marc become someone else. The smiles disappeared. He stayed tense and on edge. His gaze never stopped scanning every corner. Before the first time they kissed, Marc never stopped smiling. He laughed all the time and kept Valon distracted. Valon wasn't complaining. He loved every version of Marc. Valon just worried maybe Marc wasn't exactly as happy as Valon. Of course, this had become an issue he overthought. He had started paying closer attention to how much Marc did for him and comparing it to how much Valon gave back. The scales were uneven as hell. It was easy to get lost in the center of Marc's orbit. Marc spoiled him nonstop, and Valon took it. That was their dynamic. But Valon didn't want to be like that any longer, and he was determined to be better.

Typically, Valon loved for Marc to shower with him. He did not feel that way after concerts. Valon was a sweaty, nasty mess. Marc would never let him get clean. They had parted ways at the top of the stairs and jumped into two different showers. After a long scrub and all the good-smelling things, Valon stepped from the bathroom. He didn't know how long it would take for Marc to finish. Valon stole his chance to pull Marc's ring from the box and inspect the piece. It was a gorgeous ring. Even though Valon hadn't thought he expressed himself well, it seemed Grant had known exactly what Valon meant. Valon wasn't surprised. Grant was the highest paid and most sought-after jeweler for a reason. He was also married to a hockey player, so he understood the manly beauty Valon wanted. The band was perfect.

"Are you coming to bed, gorgeous?"

Valon nearly jumped out of his skin. He definitely dropped Marc's ring. Thankfully, it had landed at his feet and didn't budge. Valon picked it up. He turned and found Marc already under the sheets. Valon hadn't even looked that way as he left the bathroom. His mind had been on making sure he had a ring on Marc's finger before they went to sleep. Valon didn't want even a single night more to pass without knowing Marc was permanently his.

Marc stacked his hands behind his head and watched Valon with heat-filled eyes. "Damn. Look at you. No clothes. The perfect silhouette with the bathroom light behind you."

Valon hadn't thought it was possible for him to blush. Something in Marc's tone just penetrated his shamelessness. There was a tingle in Valon's stomach. Had Marc always looked so obsessed with him? Damn. It was like owning a grizzly.

Part of him was a little petrified. Yet all of him was honored to be the center of Marc's infatuation. They would have an amazing life together.

"I hope you never stop looking at me the way you are now."

Marc sat up. His eyes never budged from Valon. "Don't worry. You're the center of my universe." Marc's claim proved he knew exactly how he looked when he focused on Valon. Valon didn't know if that confession should add to the fear or the happiness. Maybe it was a little of both. Marc motioned him closer. "Come here."

Valon didn't hesitate. The second he was within reach, Marc had him pulled onto his lap. His mouth covered Valon's moan at having his bare body against Marc. He tried to bury his hand in Marc's hair. The move reminded him he held Marc's ring.

Valon pulled away for a moment. "Put this on." He shoved the ring into Marc's hand before shifting positions to straddle Marc. His intention had been to immediately steal Marc's mouth again. Instead, he watched as Marc slipped the ring onto his left hand. His face held Valon captivated. Marc looked at the piece like he witnessed a miracle. He was transfixed. Valon was too. He couldn't look away from Marc's expression. Love swelled in his chest.

"I've never wanted anything as badly as I want this." As the words left his lips, Valon realized how true they were. A lot of dreams had come true for him that other people begged for. Still, Marc was what he needed and coveted more than anything he had set his sights on. At his confession, Marc's chin shot up. His gaze collided with Valon's. Valon saw everything he felt staring back at him. He couldn't stop baring his soul. "I've been waiting my whole life for you." Valon had never meant anything more.

Marc's hands smoothed their way up Valon's back. His eyes never left Valon's face, even as he rolled and settled between Valon's thighs. The connection was powerful as hell. Marc was back to being the person who was nearly too intense for him. Valon had grown more than accustomed to the change.

"Sometimes, it's like you're two different people. One laughing goofball who brightens my life, and the guy I'm looking at right now. I'm in love with both sides of you."

Apparently, that was the right thing to say. Marc shoved one hand beneath Valon's ass, holding him in place as he shifted positions. His mouth covered Valon's as his hips rolled. The sound that came from Marc as he created friction between them was the neediest whimper Valon ever heard. He wanted more.

Marc didn't say a word. His body did all the talking. He made love to Valon. Valon felt the tender passion flowing from him. It got harder to focus on anything except the way Marc played his body. Valon felt cherished but also desired. He balanced on the edge of a knife. Valon never wanted the moment to end, but he couldn't fight the pleasure. The sensation of the way Marc moved against him and the hunger he felt in Marc's every move was too much. Valon's orgasm hit, but there was an odd peace to the moment—like a silent promise made. Then Marc's cum also filled the space between them, and Valon automatically encircled Marc's neck, trying to hang on to him. An irrational fear hit that Marc might slip away if he let go. He couldn't allow that to happen. Valon would never let anything break them.

Chapter Eleven

THE WAY MARC SLEPT nude, sheet barely covering his cock and his arm thrown across his eyes, was mesmerizing. His wide, long body was covered in hair and got Valon hot. Marc had been visibly exhausted for a while now. Valon was used to tour life. Marc was not. Valon had to let the man sleep. It was hard, though. Valon's mouth filled with saliva at just the sight of him. They had forgotten to pull the blackout drapes closed last night. The morning sun highlighted the sexiness way too much.

With an inner sigh of regret, Valon crawled out of the bed. He found a pair of pajama pants and quietly pulled the blackout curtains closed. For a moment, he stood in the middle of the sitting room area in his bedroom. Valon couldn't think of a single thing to do until Marc was up. If all else failed, he could head for the kitchen. He wasn't hungry, but he probably should eat. On his way, his eyes automatically slid toward Marc's bedroom. They had intended to move Marc's things before leaving for his tour. In fact, they had grabbed a few empty boxes. But the idea of going on vacation had won, and nothing had gotten done. Valon smiled. Most of Marc's things had migrated to Valon's room already. There wasn't much left to move. He could throw everything into boxes while Marc slept. One chore down, and his place in Valon's bed solidified.

Valon stepped inside. The boxes sat on the bed. He knew he could get his staff to take care of this, but putting effort in made the move feel special. Valon felt a little like he was snooping as he packed what was left of Marc's clothes. He scooped up a stack of t-shirts, and a book fell out, landing on his toes.

"Goddamn it. Motherfucker." He tossed the clothes toward the bed and then checked out his poor, abused foot. Damn. That shit had hurt. Blood rose to the surface. The book was less than a foot away. It was open, and a few papers had slid across the floor. He gathered the items one by one, intent on shoving them back inside the book. One was Marc's social security card. Valon didn't even give it a glance before grabbing the next thing. It was his birth certificate. It made sense that he would keep everything on hand. Marc hadn't lived in a permanent location before settling in with Valon.

Valon shoved the papers into the book. He started to close it, but something caught his eye. The name on the birth certificate was John Marcus Campbell. There was something familiar about that name. Surely Marc had told him his full name at some point. That was the only explanation that made sense. He grabbed the other scattered slips of paper. He might not have looked at them at all if he hadn't caught sight of a familiar name: Backlash. Curiosity had Valon eyeing all the papers. They were digital printouts of concert confirmation receipts. Every single one was for his group. He flipped through the book, looking for more loose papers. Every one he found was another of his concerts. Valon's brow furrowed. Marc had obviously been to dozens of his concerts all around the world. Not just in the U.S., but in England and Canada too.

Valon moved to the bed and sat. He didn't understand why he hadn't known Marc was a fan. He knew Marc liked his music, but Marc had never acted like the typical fanatic, which was how these papers made him look. Valon was too far into the mystery of things now. He didn't know what he was looking for, but he flipped through the pages again. It struck Valon. The book was a journal. Everything inside him screamed for him to put the private writings away. It was wrong to read someone's thoughts without their permission. If the shoe were on the other foot, Valon would be upset if Marc read his journal. But something just didn't feel right, and Valon didn't know why. The concert tickets were so at odds with the Marc he knew. They went back for years, since not long after Valon's first song broke the internet due to all the people trying to download his music at once. Maybe Marc hadn't wanted to make Valon uncomfortable by admitting he loved Valon's music this much. Another familiar name jumped out at him. Thacker Street. The entry was the last before the pages went blank.

9:00 a.m. to 9:30 jogs Thacker Street.

9:30 returns to his apartment inside the gym.

Thirty minutes later, the doors are unlocked to let customers in.

Valon read line after line, describing someone's day. Unfortunately, he knew exactly whose schedule it was. Ry had stringently kept the same daily pattern as long as Valon could remember. Why would Marc have this? Unless... No. His mind refused to go there. Marc was always with him. Not to mention, Valon clearly remembered looking at the clock at nine on the day Ry had been killed. Marc had brought him so much pleasure, and all Valon thought about later was how he had been making love while Ry fought for his life. There was no way Marc had done anything. They had been together. Valon flipped back to nearly the beginning of the journal. He had to focus on anything else.

I saw him tonight. He looked right through me. Of course, he did. He doesn't know I exist.

Nope. Valon couldn't read about Marc wanting someone else. He flipped forward.

I'm getting closer. Maybe we'll at least cross paths. That would likely take a miracle, though. I got the position as Ledger Stark's part-time guard. I didn't even have to ask. The odds of Valon visiting at the same time as one of my shifts are minuscule at best. But his dad seems great. He talks about Valon a lot. It's like he's there. Like I'm not a stranger.

Valon stopped reading. He stared into space. He couldn't read another word, and he definitely didn't know how he felt. This seemed like more than just being a rabid fan. Marc had obviously worked at getting close to him. Somehow, he had made his way all the way into Valon's bed. A shiver ran through Valon.

The bed dipped beside him. Marc took the book and loose papers from him. He worked quietly to set the book to rights. "I wish you hadn't read that." His dead tone had Valon incapable of looking anywhere else. Marc looked sad. Valon's chest hurt because he loved Marc, and the reason he had occasionally been a little scared of him showed itself. He never thought he would question his safety with Marc at his side. Valon definitely never expected him to need protection from Marc.

Marc flipped to a specific spot and tucked his birth certificate and social security card inside before dropping the book into the open box. His gaze never moved Valon's way. Everything inside Valon screamed for Marc to fucking look at him and tell him it was all a bad joke.

"Did you kill Ry?"

The smile that immediately stretched Marc's lips looked a bit unhinged. He chuckled. "You too, huh? Just like Kash, you think I have some predisposition to go on a murder spree just because of my dad. No, I didn't kill Ry. His death was a happy accident. His dick got him killed."

Marc moved around the room, packing his things while he spoke. "Steel sent me notes on Ry's schedule. We had a plan to discredit Ry in every way. If we ruined his life enough, we could ensure nothing he ever said would be taken seriously. We were trying to free you. Then the jackass caught sight of some guy across a busy street. German says it was beyond obvious he was headed to shoot his shot. Of course, German couldn't say for sure that's what happened. He was too far away to see the guy too clearly. But Ry being Ry, he ran right out in the road for a chance at a new fuck buddy." Marc slapped his hands together, making Valon jump. "Dead."

Valon was still too shocked to think clearly.

Marc obviously didn't need him for this conversation. He angrily tossed the last of his clothes into the box. "So, no. My dad's serial killer genes or whatever did not pass down to me. Thanks for showing me you're just like everyone else. I tried going by my middle name. For fuck's sake, I dropped out of college after the third accusation from police that whoever was the latest missing person had to be my fault somehow."

So much information landed on Valon, he didn't know what to do or say. His emotions swung wildly. "Your dad was a serial killer?"

Marc didn't answer. He snatched up the box. "I'll get out of your way. You can throw the rest of my shit away, I guess. I'm pretty sure you paid for it all anyhow despite me asking you not to do that."

Valon watched in stunned silence as Marc left. In nothing but a t-shirt and pajama pants, Marc jogged down the stairs. Valon lost sight of him around the fourth step due to the way the room was shaped. On autopilot, Valon stood and moved to the top of the stairs. He heard the chirp of the back door opening. It chirped again when it closed. Valon sat on the top step and stared at nothing. Over the years, he had been so high, he had forgotten his own name, and still Valon had never been this wiped clean. His brain refused to churn out a single coherent thought. But beneath everything, one thing still stood clear. He loved a man he didn't know, and that man had just walked out of his life.

Marc refused to think. He couldn't. His truck basically drove itself without Marc's input at all. It had been so long since Marc had driven his truck, he had to adjust to the stiff brakes again. Like every car in Valon's garage, a company came every couple of weeks to start, drive, and mechanically inspect the vehicle. Thank God. He didn't know what he would have done if his truck hadn't started. Even though he had no place to go, he knew he couldn't stay at Valon's.

Marc pulled into the first parking lot and parking spot he came to. He covered his eyes. Valon's expression stared back at him behind his closed lids. The hurt, betrayal, and fear he had seen. Marc drew a breath that sounded like he was choking. Valon had looked at him like he was a monster. He swiped his eyes and stared into space. Time passed without him. His mind completely shut down. He had flown too close to the sun and lost everything in the fire.

Marc had been incapable of staying to face the wrath. Even now, without Valon having said a single harsh word, Marc couldn't cope. What had he thought would happen? He supposed he just prayed Valon wouldn't see him for the messed-up sociopath he was. Now that hope was dead. All hope for him at all dashed upon the rocks.

The passenger-side door opened. Ledger climbed in.

Marc stared at him, too numb to react.

Ledger shook his phone at him. "You shared your location with me a while back in case I got worried about Valon. You never withdrew permission on the app, so..." Ledger shrugged.

"I remember." Holy fucking shit. Was that his voice? He sounded like he had been screaming at the top of his lungs for hours. In a way, he had been. He just hadn't made a sound.

"Kash is with Valon, since you left him unguarded."

"What are you doing here?" Marc had to look around to find out where here was. "Getting coffee?" It was Valon's favorite coffeehouse. How sad for this to be where autopilot had taken him.

"No, I'm here for you."

Marc didn't bother saying anything. If Ledger wanted to tear into him for stalking the man's son to the point of insanity, well, he was owed that. Marc was too broken to care. Plus, Ledger's eyes had been passed down to Valon. They were a perfect match, and Marc couldn't look away.

Ledger eyed him as if searching for something. Probably a soul. Marc wasn't so sure he had one of those. Finally, Ledger motioned toward the building. "I used to bring Valon here all the time. It was one of our secret trips. They weren't really secret. I just loved taking Valon shopping, getting coffee before and lunch after. I wanted him to feel as special to me as he is. It was our thing."

"I know." Marc paused for a moment. "Valon told me. That's not me stalking him." He had to add on that part because, fuck. Marc knew how things looked. They looked exactly like they were.

Weirdly, Ledger smiled. "He really told you that? I thought he had forgotten."

Marc had nothing left to lose. The least he could do was tell Ledger the truth so he could know what he had been fighting since Valon left home. "Of course he didn't forget. Those were the only times when he felt happy and safe. Ry made him pay double for him taking you away from Ry for the day."

Ledger stared at the building. He visibly swallowed. "I know. He told me."

Marc's issues took a backseat. He felt an odd kinship with Ledger. They both loved a man whom they couldn't always reach. He wished he hadn't said anything. Just as Valon had kept his secrets for decades so he wouldn't hurt his dad, Marc didn't want to hurt Ledger.

"You should hear him when he talks about you. Bad memories tend to sear deeper into our brains than good times, but Valon still talks about a lot of good times with you. I'm sure you blame yourself, but don't. That's exactly why Valon never said anything. He couldn't watch you hurt."

Ledger wrung his hands in his lap, openly fighting against the ugly things he knew now. “I’m the reason Ry is dead.” He shot Marc a desperate look. “I never want Valon to know that. But after Valon told me what he had done, I couldn’t breathe knowing he was alive. So I waited until Kash left the house for the day. I knew exactly where Ry would be, and I stood on the other side of that busy road. He had been trying so hard to get me back. So I knew all I had to do was smile and give a little wave, and I was right.”

“Good. He deserved it.”

Ledger flashed him a sad sigh. “Please don’t tell Valon. He’s been through enough.”

A humorless grunt of laughter came from Marc's throat. "No problem. He'll never speak to me again."

"You'll just have to make him, then." Ledger was all smiles now. "The only way to get through to Valon is to not leave him a choice. At least that's what's always worked for Kash. Kash just tells him how it's going to be, and Valon goes along with it. Kash thinks he only feels secure if someone else is in control while making Valon think he's in charge. I've always thought you were damn good at that. Every time we made plans, you stated things in such a way that Valon thought he had picked the time and place to see us. Honestly, it's a talent I wish you could bottle and sell."

Marc felt like his heart was actively being crushed. "You don't want me around

Valon. Didn't Kash tell you? I'm that guy who might start burying bodies in the backyard any day now."

"Why would he think that?"

Fuck. Kash hadn't told him. Of course he hadn't. Kash wouldn't want Ledger to worry. "My dad—"

Ledger immediately cut him off. "I've known all about that since the day we met. It's possible that's why you won Valon. Maybe something about you let him know you'd understand. You know what it's like to be scarred by a parent. It's probably nice knowing he's not alone."

"You've always known?" Marc didn't mean to sound so accusatory, but damn. He had never let on he knew a thing about Marc.

Ledger's hands rose and fell. "After Ry, it's possible I'm a horrible judge of character. I don't think I'm wrong about you, though. When you look at Valon, all I see is how deeply you love him. As a father, you can't know how good that makes me feel, knowing my son has the love I've always wanted for him." Ledger visibly swallowed again. "Please don't walk away without trying. I don't know what'll happen to Valon without you. He needs you."

Marc wasn't sure what would happen to him if he tried and failed. Walking away, making a clean break without hearing Valon say he hated Marc, that felt like the safest decision for his barely existent sanity. But Marc's lips wouldn't shape the word no. "I'm coming back to haunt you if he kills me."

A low rumble of laughter rolled from Ledger's side of the truck. "Deal."

Marc rubbed his forehead, wondering what the hell he had just agreed to do. Truth be told, he didn't know if he was strong enough. He would find out nonetheless.

Chapter Twelve

It seemed like it should be odd that Valon called Kash first. Kash was the first thought he had the moment Marc walked out. But as he sat tucked beneath Kash's arm, Valon realized something. He had always leaned on Kash as more of a second father. Kash had always been so damn solid and grown that Valon had seen a place of safety and comfort in him. He had always known, no matter how furious Kash might be with him at any given time, he could call Kash and he would be there.

Valon didn't talk. Kash didn't make him. They just sat together in silence, with Kash shoring him up. His mind raced in a dozen directions but refused to cling to a single topic. If he stopped and focused on any one thing, Valon would fall apart. Nothing held him together other than his shocked state.

Occasionally, Kash would kiss his temple and give him a little squeeze. He was the dad who didn't judge, pry, or feel like if he said nothing then he wasn't actively solving the problem. Kash was exactly who he needed. Maybe when his head cleared, he would feel guilty for not calling his real dad. He hoped his dad wasn't hurt that Valon called Kash. It was just that everything hurt too fucking badly, and if a single person gave a shred of sympathy or advice, Valon would fall apart.

A noise in the doorway snagged his attention. His gaze turned away from his inward stare. Marc stood in the foyer, shifting from foot to foot. He looked so adorably unsure.

Kash kissed his temple again. “I’m always a call or text away.”

Valon managed a sad smile. “I know.”

Kash stood. He nodded at Marc as he passed on his way to the door. Marc’s gaze never looked away from Valon to acknowledge Kash.

Valon didn’t react the second they were alone. It took him a minute to find his voice in the face of Marc’s open pain.

He cleared his throat, hoping he didn't sound as much like he was drowning. "Is your plan to stand there all day?"

Marc didn't move. "I'm waiting to see if you tell me to leave."

"Then come sit down."

Marc's broken expression never budged. He chose a seat across the coffee table from Valon. Even when he sat, he didn't relax. Marc looked ready to run again at any second.

"I'm not my dad." Marc jutted out his chin, as if preparing for Valon not to believe.

"I have no fucking clue who your dad is." Valon heard the barely contained pain in his voice.

Marc relaxed a tad, but not much. He didn't look as if he believed Valon. "Everything I told you about my childhood and parents was true. I never lied. I grew up middle class, never going without but also not having the latest things. My life was completely normal. I was the typical teenager. We were a white-picket-fence family. Cookie-cutter as hell. Then one day my mom opened the door to what looked like an entire police station and half the FBI."

"That sounds terrifying." Valon didn't know what else to say, but he needed Marc to know he listened. He had to do something. Otherwise, they would never get anywhere.

Marc nodded. "We had no clue what was happening. I was seventeen. One second, I was a normal high school senior. The next thing I knew, I was in an interrogation room completely shut off from everyone I loved. They kept tossing questions at me about things that didn't make sense. I was sick with fear and confusion."

"That's a terrible thing to do to a kid." Even Valon heard the outrage in his voice.

A small smile passed over Marc's lips before disappearing just as quickly. "I'm pretty sure they didn't see me as a kid. But I felt like one, and it was a nightmare. They were showing me horrific pictures and screaming questions at me. Nothing made sense."

Marc dropped his gaze to his clasped hands resting on his lap. His knuckles were white. "That's the day I found out my dad is the Tower Highway killer."

Valon covered his mouth. That was why Marc's name sounded familiar. He had the same name as his dad. Marc had actually said his dad was a serial killer before he left, but Valon had been too upset to absorb every word.

Marc cocked his head to one side and studied Valon. "You really didn't know."

Valon shook his head even though he was seventy-five percent certain it hadn't been a question.

A wry smile touched Marc's lips. "You didn't know, and you still asked if I killed Ry. Fair, I guess. My journal probably made me look pretty psycho."

Valon needed to know everything. Apparently, he had been self-absorbed and never asked any real questions about Marc or his life. Now he couldn't stop wondering why he had done that. "Are you?"

Marc's hands rose and fell. He looked defeated. "I don't know. Maybe. It's entirely possible Dad passed some horrible genes down to me. I just..." His hands rose and fell again. "My mom killed herself after the trial. Everyone was gone from my life, and cops kept showing up at my door, year after year, questioning me about missing people. It was like everyone thought I followed in Dad's footsteps. I had to drop out of college and move away. When Steel hired me and gave me the chance to keep moving, I found my first ounce of peace in years. Then your song 'Broken People' hit the charts, and I swear I could've written every word. You hit me right in the heart, giving me a voice when I didn't have one.

Then I don't know. I went to every concert I could. It's dumb, but you made me feel less alone. I'd watch you sing that song, and I knew. That song was your life too." Marc's expression shifted from desperate to hopeful. "Then the job to protect your dad on Kash's days off came available. I didn't even get a chance to request the position. Steel just gave it to me. It felt almost serendipitous—like we were meant to meet. Then we did, and I realized I had been right. You were broken just like me. Instantly, I knew I had to save you." Marc's eyes turned pleading. "I swear I never set out to be anything more than your friend. Trust me, I know exactly how bad this looks and how insane I sound. I would run from me in your shoes. In fact, after I kissed you, I debated whether I should just get in my truck and go. That's how much I've never wanted you to think this was my plan all along. Nothing has been faked or contrived. But yeah, the closer I got to you, the more I wanted. But that's because you're fucking amazing, and not because of who you are. Please don't hate me for connecting with a star who wrote my life into song. It's you I fell in love with, and I've lived in fear every single day since that this exact thing would happen. I'll do whatever you need, but please don't look at me in fear the way you did earlier. The way you're doing now."

Something shook loose inside Valon while watching Marc beg. The clouds parted. He knew what roiled inside him. "I'm not scared. That's not what you're seeing. I'm fucking furious." In his rage, Valon came to his feet and paced. "You just walked out. I was shocked by what I found and even more surprised and confused when you got angry with me for it." His pacing became an even more furious motion. He smacked the back of his hand against his other palm as he made his points. "The person who'd just agreed to marry me walked out. No trying to talk it out." He smacked his palm again. "No waiting to let me think for a second. Just gone." Valon faced Marc so he could see his rage. "We were supposed to get married. How am I supposed to feel now? Did you just show me how little that word means to you? I believe marriages are forever. You agreed to forever and then just fucking left me." Valon had been so beaten down throughout his life, he had lived in fear of showing this much anger. The fire left him. Sadness replaced the fury.

"You're the love I spent my entire life begging for. Did it ever occur to you that maybe I need someone who is infatuated with me for once? Not someone who wants someone else or can't take being around when the chips are down. Maybe I crave that all-consuming passion. I believed with my entire soul that you would never hurt me, and you did. You made me trust you above everyone else, and then you just took a sledgehammer to that foundation. You were supposed to be different." The anguish in his voice couldn't be missed. Valon had genuinely believed Marc loved him, and then Marc took his affection away. He didn't know how to face that.

Marc visibly swallowed. His arresting eyes never wavered from Valon's face. "Why are you talking in past tense?"

Valon's hands rose and fell. A hysterical-sounding laugh escaped him. "You tell me. You're the one who quit us."

In an instant, Marc was on his feet and across the room so fast, Valon didn't have time to run. He was in Marc's arms, and the hottest kiss possible stole his breath.

Marc pulled away and rested his forehead on Valon's. Their faces were inches apart. Marc's eyes somehow looked even more beautiful up close. "I'm sorry. In every way possible, I'm ashamed as hell of myself. You're right. I should've stayed. There's no excuse. It was like some sort of fucked-up PTSD response, and you didn't deserve that. Please forgive me. I swear it'll never happen again." The sadness and desperation couldn't be missed in Marc's voice. "When I left here, I had no destination in mind. I didn't even get that far. My mind just undermined me, but as soon as even a hair of the fog cleared, I knew I had fucked up. I remembered there was no way in hell I could live without you. Please believe in me again. Please believe in us."

Valon stared at the other half of his soul. Marc was right to connect so fiercely with that song. It was about people like them. He was convinced they had been meant to find each other.

"I don't care what drove you to me. It doesn't matter. You brought exactly the insanity I need to survive. I just want us."

The relief and love in Marc's eyes told the entire story. He would never regret them. Marc wouldn't let him. When they had met, Valon had been at the lowest point of his life. Marc had saved him, and Valon knew he would never let Valon hurt again. He needed the obsessive love he had read about in that book. Valon thought he might actually die without it.

Marc's stomach shook. When he had come home, he hadn't known what would happen. He hadn't known what to say or do. As always, Valon had the words. Valon could say all the things Marc couldn't string together. His rage turned out to the exact thing Marc needed.

"I love you." Marc's voice cracked, and he didn't care. "You have no fucking idea how much."

Tears slipped down Valon's cheeks. They shattered Marc's heart. Marc swiped them away. "Please don't cry. I hate that I hurt you."

Valon drew a broken breath. "These are tears of terror. You're not supposed to go away."

Marc couldn't take it. He swept Valon off his feet and carried him to the couch. He sat with Valon on his lap and grabbed a nearby throw blanket to cover them. Marc held Valon as tightly as he could, hoping to squeeze the fear and pain from him. His throat swelled. He had done more damage than he realized by walking out. Marc had been totally convinced Valon wouldn't want him anymore after seeing that journal. All Marc had known was he couldn't stay and watch Valon rip his love away. He couldn't watch the love turn to hate. But now he saw everything, and the guilt was massive. He had saved Valon and loved him through his mental downfall. Watching Marc leave had to have felt like the ultimate betrayal. Marc had no idea how to fix it, but Valon still wanted him, and Marc would find a way to scrub away this day.

"We'll sit here until you believe in me again."

Valon pressed his face against Marc's neck, snuggling closer. "My insides are shaking, and I'm scared to move."

Marc kept him as secure as possible. “So don’t. I’m not going anywhere.”

Valon sniffed and then chuckled. “This’ll get really awkward when one of us has to pee.”

A smile exploded across Marc’s face. “Do you have any suggestions on how to get around that?”

“We could go sit like this in the shower and just let it fly.”

A bark of laughter burst from him. “Ewww.”

The way Valon shook with laughter felt amazing against his chest. “What? You don’t get peed on every day?”

Marc snorted. “You can aim away from me from your position. It’s more likely you’ll be the one getting pissed on.” He couldn't stop smiling. It was such a dumb conversation. So typically them.

Valon's smile could be felt against his neck. "What is wrong with us?"

Nothing. That thought hit hard. There was absolutely fucking nothing wrong with them. They were flawless together. "We're too much alike."

"Impossible." Valon's immediate response made Marc snuggle closer, settling in for the long haul. Valon stroked his collarbone. "We should do something really crazy and make this entire morning vanish."

"Just tell me what and I'm in. As long as I'm with you, nothing matters. Let's build a rock formation of our names together so it can be seen from the sky. We could have landscaping mow the words into the grass, or plant flowers in that shape. Help me out here. I'm trying to think of something harmless but beautiful." Marc had a lot of outlandish ideas, but he didn't want Valon to think their conversation had gone too far.

Valon kissed his neck. "We could get married today."

Everything inside Marc froze for a second while he absorbed the suggestion. His cheeks hurt, making him realize how big he smiled. "Yes. I love it. Let's get married today." Now that the words were out there, the true excitement set in. He wanted this. In fact, Marc more than wanted them to get married. He needed it to happen. Maybe the shaking and fear would go away. The knowledge that Valon was legally his would soothe the insane and greedy beast inside him.

Valon didn't leap from his lap or cheer. He kept stroking Marc's collarbone and snuggling. "I'd love for you to take my last name."

Tears rushed to Marc's eyes. He fought them. "There's nothing I'd rather do." Marc sounded as moved as he was. He couldn't help it. Marc had chosen to go by a shortened version of his middle name to distance himself from his dad. He had been scared to legally change his entire name for fear of drawing attention to himself with the media. Plus, his dad still sat on death row. Since it turned out he didn't really know the man, he didn't know how he would react to Marc changing his name. It was possible that even a cage couldn't hold his evil if Marc denounced him, taking away his trophy. Maybe he would find a way to hurt him, which was still such an odd thought. His dad had never laid a finger on him or as much as yelled at his mom. To this day, finding out he had been raised by a monster felt so unreal. He couldn't bring himself to believe his dad didn't love him, and he wasn't sure John Campbell was capable of love. Maybe he just mimicked feelings. Marc had no idea. But in his heart, he knew if a name change came by marrying someone as amazing as Valon, he would be proud rather than offended. Marc knew it was such a horrible way of looking at things, but how was he supposed to feel? No one had helped him deal. They only looked at him with disgust, suspicion, and fear. No one had worried about his mental health. But Valon offering him his last name was such a beautiful proposal and moving as hell.

No matter what happened from this moment on, Marc would love and cherish Valon for the rest of their lives, likely even beyond this life.

Chapter Thirteen

PLAYING THE BODYGUARD NEVER stopped. After the training, the years of work, and actively saving people occasionally, the eyes automatically sought every dark corner, focusing on every passing face. Sometimes German even caught himself memorizing tag numbers. He always expected the worst. Maybe that was why it surprised him so much to watch Marc marry Valon. To him, they had felt very unlikely to make it. Not only was Valon a notorious brat most guards refused to get anywhere near, but they had planned to ruin one of Valon's dads. Granted, Dad was a loose, undeserved title, and the guy had been a horrible person; sometimes the heart didn't care about any of that shit. Your father was your father, and that could cause some complicated as fuck feelings when the parent did terrible things. While, in the end, Marc had done nothing wrong to the man, German had still expected the entire situation would bite him in the end. Somehow, no. They had looked fiercely serious while exchanging vows, and their smiles had been huge when they were announced as spouses for life. Sometimes life brought together the strangest pairings. It was kind of nice.

A muscular figure moved his way. The string of lights twinkling above the pool highlighted the gray in Steel's salt and pepper hair. Steel had always been a mystery to him. He treated every one of his employees like family. He was always there when anyone needed him. But German sometimes wondered if Steel had a single actual friend. There was something about him that felt untouchable—almost as if his entire personality was a veneer no one saw beneath.

He smiled as he handed German a glass of champagne. "Why do I always find you in a corner?"

German avoided the question. "This is one hell of a nice wedding and reception to have gotten thrown together in a few hours."

Steel let the dodge stand. He shrugged, making his custom-made suit highlight his muscles for a second. "Money moves mountains. You know this. We see it every day in our business."

He supposed that was true. "I guess something about this one seemed especially rushed but still somehow perfect. So, I'm guessing you're feeling pretty proud of yourself. First, Kash and Ledger. Now, Marc and Valon. You're becoming quite the matchmaker."

Steel tossed him a wink before downing his champagne.

Someone jostled German from behind, falling into him. Blaze, the drummer of Valon's band, moved past him, all drunken smiles. "Sorry about that, my guy. Didn't see you there."

German bit back his annoyance. Valon's drummer was also a client. He had to stay polite. "No worries. Six foot five is practically invisible." Blaze barked out a laugh. "Yeah. For sure. Everyone's getting lit in the pool house if you're in."

German fought to hang on to his smile. Blaze was young, especially compared to German. He had unbelievable talent and a life most would kill to have. Yet, just like every rockstar before him, he threw everything away for drugs.

"Less for me means more for you. Have fun."

Blaze winked and turned away, getting carried away by a sea of men. He would probably fuck every single one of them by the end of the night. German blew out a sigh. He missed guarding Jathan. That had been a quiet job.

Steel slapped German on the shoulder and squeezed, grabbing his attention. “You’d best watch out. Maybe I’ll doom you to a life of happiness next. Anyhow, enjoy yourself. I’m headed out.”

German looked around. “Already? They haven’t even cut the cake or anything.”

Steel’s silver eyes danced with humor. “Yeah. The grooms sneaked away a good half an hour ago. It’s just a party now. We won’t see those guys again.”

“Well, damn.” German had kind of wanted to congratulate Marc. He was one of the few guards German saw as a friend.

With a laugh, Steel wandered away with his hands in his jacket pockets. Alone.

The way he always was. German kind of felt a little sad for him, and he didn't know why.

"I happened to think."

German startled at the loud, slurred words. Blaze was back.

"You didn't tell me your name."

German had no idea why he was smiling. Everything about the situation just seemed humorous. "You didn't ask."

Blaze hummed. "I see. A smart-ass. I'm Blaze and you are..."

German's smile got brighter. "German."

"Cool. Now we know each other. Let's go."

With no clue how it happened, German found Blaze's arm linked through his, dragging him away. For some reason he couldn't place, he was having a good time. He still couldn't stop smiling. German used Steel's solitude as a lesson to choose life. No one was meant to be alone, and everyone only lived once.

Valon tore at Marc's clothes. Marc fought to catch his breath from all the excitement. They both laughed as they left a trail of clothes behind them on the way to the bedroom. Their horrible morning felt like a lifetime ago. They had done this crazy thing and tied their lives together forever with next to no planning. Their kiss was aggressive. Marc couldn't get close enough to Valon to appease his heart. He took Valon down onto the mattress like he physically attacked him. Valon came back just as rough. His short fingernails dug into Marc's skin.

Marc tore his mouth away and panted. The knowledge that he had married the center of his obsession was all-consuming. He couldn't get inside Valon quickly enough. "I need you."

"I love you." Valon's gasped words had Marc grabbing the lube where they left it last night.

Marc responded while he worked, lubing Valon's asshole. "I love you so fucking much." He couldn't wait any longer. Marc pushed his way inside. "Fuck." Marc couldn't stop the groaned curse. If he could never stop being joined with Valon, Marc would do it. Every time they made love, he wanted more before he even got fully started. His body was as greedy as his heart. He pumped inside Valon hard and fast until reality hit again. Marc slowed and savored the man who belonged to him now.

"The way you look at me is addictive. I can tell how much you want only me by your eyes alone."

Marc changed angles. Valon shouldn't be so coherent.

Valon moaned and visibly fought his way toward the edge. "Please, baby. I want to drip with your cum."

Marc's crazed emotions doubled. Valon begged for him. Him. His emotions grew to an uncontainable level. No matter how hard he tried, Marc couldn't go slow tonight. He needed to mark his territory. Marc nipped every place he could reach as he took Valon so hard, heavy breathing and slapping skin were the only noises in the room, broken only by the occasional moan or plea. Valon tensed beneath him. Marc focused on every tiny detail. He didn't want to forget a single thing about this night. When Valon came, Marc changed angles again and rode his orgasm. Marc's entire body stiffened in anticipation. He blew, crying Valon's name.

Valon sucked a spot on Marc's chest while Marc whined his way through the gut-wrenching pleasure. As the air began to cool his skin, Marc shifted positions and cuddled Valon. His lips still didn't want to leave Valon's skin.

Time passed while they savored their new existence. Valon was the first one to speak. "Do you think Dad will be pissed we left our own reception?"

Marc chuckled. The laugh sounded tired even to him. "Judging by the looks he kept exchanging with Kash, I doubt he's noticed."

Another silent moment passed. Guilt set in. Ledger and Kash had immediately returned to the house when Valon and he decided to marry that night. They had worked hard, calling people and getting everything arranged. Marc shouldn't have pulled Valon away from everyone celebrating them.

"We could always clean up, change clothes, and return like that had been our intention all along."

The way Valon carefully made the suggestion, as if he didn't want to disappoint Marc, had Marc jumping right in to do anything Valon wanted. "We should do that. I want to look back on tonight and have tons of memories."

They rushed through getting ready. While Marc helped clean Valon's body, an image of their future ran through his mind. Things would be exactly like this for the rest of his life. Every pointless dream he had ever dared to imagine had come true. He was floored all over again by the blessings he had been handed.

“You know I meant every word, right?” Marc’s question came out soft yet serious. “Every single vow.”

“I didn’t.” Valon’s response stopped Marc’s heart. “I have no intention of letting death take anything from me.”

Relief had the blood returning to his brain so quickly, his head spun. Valon wrapped his arms around Marc’s neck. “You’re not getting away from me that easily. I’ll either haunt you or meet you in the next life. You’re mine.”

Marc’s throat swelled. He had never stared into the face of so much love. He desperately wanted to keep it forever. “You have a deal.”

A soft knock landed on the door. Ledger spoke through the wood. "Are you two coming back or should I try to wind things down out here?"

Smiles exploded across their faces.

"We'll be down in a minute." Valon yelled the answer without ever looking away from Marc. "Let's go, beautiful. We're one new set of clothes away from champagne."

Marc kissed the tip of Valon's nose. "In." Not only for champagne but for eternity. He had prepped for this for years. Now he planned to ensure Valon benefited from every crazed desire Marc had begged the universe to share with Valon. It seemed insanity had some perks.

Keep an eye out for the next Steel Security, *Just in Time*.

About the Author

Charity Parkerson is an award-winning and multi-published author with several companies. Born with no filter from her brain to her mouth, she decided to take this odd quirk and insert it in her characters. One of her greatest loves is writing morally gray characters. You'll find them scattered throughout her hundreds of titles.

*Nine-time Readers' Favorite Award Winner

*2015 Passionate Plume Award Finalist

*2013 Reviewers' Choice Award Winner

*2012 ARRA Finalist for Favorite Paranormal Romance

*Five-time winner of The Mistress of the Darkpath

Connect with her online:

*Sign up for her newsletter: https://bit.ly/charityparkersonnewsletter

*Join her readers' group on Facebook: http://bit.ly/CharitysTribe

*Website: https://www.charityparkerson.com

*A list of her social media accounts and giveaways all in one place: http://hy.page/charityparkerson

www.ingramcontent.com/pod-product-compliance
Lightning Source LLC
LaVergne TN
LVHW010643110826
845149LV00014B/2938